Fantasy Stories

Selected and edited by
Andrew Goodwyn

Oxford University Press

Oxford University Press, Walton Street, Oxford OX2 6DP

Oxford New York Toronto
Delhi Bombay Calcutta Madras Karachi
Petaling Jaya Singapore Hong Kong Tokyo
Nairobi Dar es Salaam Cape Town
Melbourne Auckland

and associated companies in
Berlin Ibadan

Oxford is a trade mark of Oxford University Press

Second impression 1992

ISBN 0 19 831262 8

The cover illustration is by Duncan Storr

Typeset by Pentacor PLC, High Wycombe, Bucks
Printed in Great Britain by
Cambridge University Press

Contents

Acknowledgements

The editor and publisher are grateful for permission to include the following copyright material.

J.G. Ballard: 'The Garden of Time' reprinted from *The Voices of Time* by permission of Victor Gollancz Ltd. **Ray Bradbury**: 'The Fog Horn' from *The Collected Stories*. First published in the *Saturday Evening Post* (The Curtis Publishing Co, 1951). © 1951, renewed 1979 by Ray Bradbury. Reprinted by permission of Don Congdon Associates, Inc. **Margaret Elphinstone**: 'Spinning the Green' reprinted from *Despatches from the Frontiers of the Female Mind* (The Women's Press Ltd, 1985). Copyright Margaret Elphinstone. **Ursula Le Guin**: 'The Wife's Story' from *The Compass Rose* (Gollancz, 1983). Reprinted by permission of A.P. Watt Limited on behalf of Ursula Le Guin. **Anne McCaffrey**: 'The Smallest Dragonboy'. Copyright © 1973 by Anne McCaffrey. First appeared in *Science Fiction Tales*. Reprinted by permission of the author and the author's agent, Virginia Kidd. **Diana L. Paxson**: 'The Mist on the Moor' reprinted from *Sword and Sorceress* Vol III (Headline, 1988) by permission of Carnell Literary Agency. **Ruth Rendell**: 'The Green Road to Quephanda' from *The New Girl Friend and Other Stories* (Hutchinson). © Kingsmarkham Enterprises Ltd 1985. Reprinted by permission of the Peters Fraser & Dunlop Group Ltd. **Jack Ritchie**: 'Kid Cardula'. First published in Alfred Hitchcock's Mystery Magazine, © 1976 by Davis Publications. Reprinted by permission of Larry Sternig Literary Agency. **Karl Edward Wagner**: 'Sing A Last Song of Valdese' reprinted from *Night Winds* by permission of Carnell Literary Agency. **Margaret Weis**: from *Dragonlance Legends, Volume 3: Test of the Twins*, by Margaret Weis and Tracy Hickman (Penguin Books, 1987), copyright © TSR Inc., 1986. Reprinted by permission of Penguin Books Ltd.

Although every effort has been made to obtain reprint permission prior to publication this has not always proved possible. Full acknowledgement has been given to author, title, source and copyright holder where known and if contacted the publisher will rectify any errors or omissions at the earliest opportunity.

Preface

One of the appeals of Fantasy is that it refuses to be tied down by a limiting definition. It is a genre in its own right, as any trip to a library or bookshop will confirm, but it has strong links with science fiction and horror and blurs into many others, including traditional Literature with a capital L. For many younger readers, however, Fantasy does have simple and clear characteristics deriving from stories of heroes and heroines often set in a magical and mythical country where good and evil struggle and we know whose side we are on. However, this is only one thread in the Fantasy weave and the following collection aims to show how many and varied are its strands.

It was once a reasonably fair criticism to say that fantasy writing was dominated by tales of male action and adventure and the cause was simple: men wrote it and men and boys read it. A glance at the contents list of this collection will disprove the point about authorship. Whilst action and violence in the physical sense play a part, many of the stories address themselves to issues of gender in a serious and subtle way and, far from having a masculine bias, they actually subvert it. There are now many female fantasy writers and the subject matter of all fantasy writers is generally much broader with an increasingly balanced readership. I hope this collection will play a part in ensuring a wider readership in the future.

The stories included here represent some of the best and most intelligent of magical and science fantasy. They are bound to attract readers who are already interested in this area of fiction but they will also help new readers to appreciate its diversity and breadth. These stories offer quite unusual kinds of reading experience and make considerable demands on the reader. Although I hope students will want to take this anthology away to read by themselves, the follow on and study suggestions are as important as in any other literary collection. Teachers and students will benefit from close analysis and discussion of each story and the whole collection provides an excellent range of writing models.

The anthology is organized so that the stories can be read without interruption. At the back is a section with follow up ideas focusing on many of the important areas outlined for GCSE and National Curriculum English. These include some biographical details on authors, some ideas for discussion and then suggestions for pair and group work, ideas for writing, extended activities and finally further reading. I hope this will be useful to teachers working with their classes and students reading the anthology alone.

Andrew Goodwyn

The Garden of Time

J. G. Ballard

Towards evening, when the great shadow of the Palladian villa filled the terrace, Count Axel left his library and walked down the wide rococo steps among the time flowers. A tall, imperious figure in a black velvet jacket, a gold tie-pin glinting below his George V beard, cane held stiffly in a white-gloved hand, he surveyed the exquisite crystal flowers without emotion, listening to the sounds of his wife's harpsichord, as she played a Mozart rondo in the music room, echo and vibrate through the translucent petals.

The garden of the villa extended for some two hundred yards below the terrace, sloping down to a miniature lake spanned by a white bridge, a slender pavilion on the opposite bank. Axel rarely ventured as far as the lake; most of the time flowers grew in a small grove just below the terrace, sheltered by the high wall which encircled the estate. From the terrace he could see over the wall to the plain beyond, a continuous expanse of open ground that rolled in great swells to the horizon, where it rose slightly before finally dipping from sight. The plain surrounded the house on all sides, its drab emptiness emphasizing the seclusion and mellowed magnificence of the villa. Here, in the garden, the air seemed brighter, the sun warmer, while the plain was always dull and remote.

As was his custom before beginning his evening stroll, Count Axel looked out across the plain to the final rise, where the horizon was illuminated like a distant stage by the fading sun. As the Mozart chimed delicately around him, flowing from his wife's graceful hands, he saw that the advance column of an enormous army was moving slowly over the horizon. At first glance, the long ranks seemed to be progressing in orderly lines, but on closer inspection, it was apparent that, like the obscured detail of Goya landscape, the army was composed of a vast throng of people, men and women, interspersed with a few soldiers in ragged uniforms, pressing forward in a disorganized tide. Some laboured under heavy loads suspended from crude yokes around their necks, others struggled with cumbersome wooden carts, their hands wrenching at the wheel spokes, a few trudged on alone, but all moved on at the same pace, bowed backs illuminated in the fleeting sun.

The advancing throng was almost too far away to be visible, but even as Axel watched, his expression aloof yet observant, it came perceptibly nearer, the vanguard of an immense rabble appearing from below the horizon. At last, as the daylight began to fade, the front edge of the throng reached the crest of the first swell below the horizon, and Axel turned from the terrace and walked down among the time flowers.

The flowers grew to a height of about six feet, their slender stems, like rods of glass, bearing a dozen leaves, the once transparent fronds frosted by the fossilized veins. At the peak of each stem was the time flower, the size of a goblet, the opaque outer petals enclosing the crystal heart. Their diamond brilliance contained a thousand faces, the crystal seeming to drain the air of its light and motion. As the flowers swayed slightly in the evening air, they glowed like flame-tipped spears.

Many of the stems no longer bore flowers, and Axel examined them all carefully, a note of hope now and then crossing his eyes as he searched for any further buds. Finally he selected a large flower on the stem nearest the wall, removed his gloves and with his strong fingers snapped it off.

As he carried the flower back on to the terrace, it began to sparkle and deliquesce, the light trapped within the core at last released. Gradually the crystal dissolved, only the outer petals remaining intact, and the air around Axel became bright and vivid, charged with slanting rays that flared away into the waning sunlight. Strange shifts momentarily transformed the evening, subtly altering its dimensions of time and space. The darkened portico of the house, its patina of age stripped away, loomed with a curious spectral whiteness as if suddenly remembered in a dream.

Raising his head, Axel peered over the wall again. Only the farthest rim of the horizon was lit by the sun, and the great throng, which before had stretched almost a quarter of the way across the plain, had now receded to the horizon, the entire concourse abruptly flung back in a reversal of time, and appeared to be stationary.

The flower in Axel's hand had shrunk to the size of a glass thimble, the petals contracting around the vanishing core. A faint sparkle flickered from the centre and extinguished itself, and Axel felt the flower melt like an ice-cold bead of dew in his hand.

Dusk closed across the house, sweeping its long shadows over the plain, the horizon merging into the sky. The harpsichord was silent, and the time flowers, no longer reflecting its music, stood motionlessly, like an embalmed forest.

For a few minutes Axel looked down at them, counting the flowers which remained, then greeted his wife as she crossed the terrace, her brocade evening dress rustling over the ornamental tiles.

'What a beautiful evening, Axel.' She spoke feelingly, as if she were thanking her husband personally for the great ornate shadow across the lawn and the dark brilliant air. Her face was serene and intelligent, her hair, swept back behind her head into a jewelled clasp, touched with silver. She wore her dress low across her breast, revealing a long slender neck and high chin. Axel surveyed her with fond pride. He gave her his arm and together they walked down the steps into the garden.

'One of the longest evenings this summer,' Axel confirmed, adding: 'I picked a perfect flower, my dear, a jewel. With luck it should last us for several days.' A frown touched his brow, and he glanced involuntarily at the wall. 'Each time now they seem to come nearer.'

His wife smiled at him encouragingly and held his arm more tightly.

Both of them knew that the time garden was dying.

Three evenings later, as he had estimated (though sooner than he secretly hoped), Count Axel plucked another flower from the time garden.

When he first looked over the wall the approaching rabble filled the distant half of the plain, stretching across the horizon in an unbroken mass. He thought he could hear the low, fragmentary sounds of voices carried across the empty air, a sullen murmur punctuated by cries and shouts, but quickly told himself that he had imagined them. Luckily, his wife was at the harpsichord, and the rich contrapuntal patterns of a Bach fugue cascaded lightly across the terrace, masking any other noises.

Between the house and the horizon the plain was divided into four huge swells, the crest of each one clearly visible in the slanting light. Axel had promised himself that he would never count them, but the number was too small to remain unobserved, particularly when it so obviously marked the progress of the advancing army. By now the forward line had passed the first crest and was well on its way to the second; the main bulk of the throng pressed behind it, hiding the crest and the even vaster concourse spreading from the horizon. Looking to left and right of the central body, Axel could see the apparently limitless extent of the army. What has seemed at first to be the central mass was no more than a minor advance guard, one of many similar arms reaching across the plain. The true centre had not yet emerged, but from the rate of extension Axel estimated that when it finally reached the plain it would completely cover every foot of ground.

Axel searched for any large vehicles or machines, but all was amorphous and unco-ordinated as ever. There were no banners or flags, no mascots or pike-bearers. Heads bowed, the multitude pressed on unaware of the sky.

Suddenly, just before Axel turned away, the forward edge of the throng appeared on top of the second crest, and swarmed down across the plain. What astounded Axel was the incredible distance it had covered while out of sight. The figures were now twice the size, each one clearly within sight.

Quickly, Axel stepped from the terrace, selected a time flower from the garden and tore it from the stem. As it released its compacted light, he returned to the terrace. When the flower had shrunk to a frozen pearl in his palm he looked out at the plain, with relief saw that the army had retreated to the horizon again.

Then he realized that the horizon was much nearer than previously, and that what he assumed to be the horizon was the first crest.

When he joined the Countess on their evening walk he told her nothing of this, but she could see behind his casual unconcern and did what she could to dispel his worry.

Walking down the steps, she pointed to the time garden. 'What a wonderful display, Axel. There are so many flowers still.'

Axel nodded, smiling to himself at his wife's attempt to reassure him. Her use of 'still' had revealed her own unconscious anticipation of the end. In fact a mere dozen flowers remained of the many hundred that had grown in the garden, and several of these were little more than buds – only three or four were fully grown. As they walked down to the lake, the Countess's dress rustling across the cool turf, he tried to decide whether to pick the larger flowers first or leave them to the end. Strictly, it would be better to give the smaller flowers additional time to grow and mature, and this advantage would be lost if he retained the larger flowers to the end, as he wished to do, for the final repulse. However, he realized that it mattered little either way; the garden would soon die and the smaller flowers required far longer than he could give them to accumulate their compressed cores of time. During his entire lifetime he had failed to notice a single evidence of growth among the flowers. The larger blooms had always been mature, and none of the buds had shown the slightest development.

Crossing the lake, he and his wife looked down at their reflections in the still black water. Shielded by the pavilion on one side and the high garden wall on the other, the villa in the distance, Axel felt composed and secure, the plain with its encroaching multitude a nightmare from which he had safely awakened. He put one arm around his wife's smooth waist and pressed her affectionately to his shoulder, realizing that he had not embraced her for several years, though their lives together had been timeless and he could remember as if yesterday when he first brought her to live in the villa.

'Axel,' his wife asked with sudden seriousness, 'before the garden dies . . . may I pick the last flower?'

Understanding her request, he nodded slowly.

One by one the succeeding evenings, he picked the remaining flowers, leaving a single small bud which grew just below the terrace for his wife. He took the flowers at random, refusing to count or ration them, plucking two or three of the smaller buds at the same time when necessary. The approaching horde had now reached the second and third crests, a vast concourse of labouring humanity that blotted out the horizon. From the terrace Axel could see clearly the shuffling, straining ranks moving down into the hollow towards the final crest, and occasionally the sounds of their voices carried across to him, interspersed with cries of anger and the cracking of whips. The wooden carts lurched from side to side on tilting wheels, their drivers struggling to control them. As far as Axel could tell, not a single member of the throng was aware of its overall direction. Rather, each one blindly moved forward across the ground directly below the heels of the person in front of him, and the only unity was that of the cumulative compass. Pointlessly, Axel hoped that the true centre, below the horizon, might be moving in a different direction, and that gradually the multitude would alter course, swing away from the villa and recede from the plain like a turning tide.

On the last evening but one, as he plucked the time flower, the forward edge of the rabble had reached the third crest, and was swarming past it. While he waited for the Countess, Axel looked at the two flowers left, both small buds which would carry them back through only a few minutes of the next evening. The glass stems of the dead flowers reared up stiffly into the air, but the whole garden had lost its bloom.

Axel passed the next morning quietly in his library, sealing the rarer of his manuscripts into the glass-topped cases between the galleries. He walked slowly down the portrait corridor, polishing each of the pictures carefully, then tidied his desk and locked the door behind him. During the afternoon he busied himself in the drawing rooms, unobtrusively assisting his wife as she cleaned their ornaments and straightened the vases and busts.

By evening, as the sun fell behind the house, they were both tired and dusty, and neither had spoken to the other all day. When his wife moved towards the music-room, Axel called her back.

'Tonight we'll pick the flowers together, my dear,' he said to her evenly. 'One for each of us.'

He peered only briefly over the wall. They could hear, less than half a mile away, the great dull roar of the ragged army, the ring of iron and lash, pressing towards the house.

Quickly, Axel plucked his flower, a bud no bigger than a sapphire. As it flickered softly, the tumult outside momentarily receded, then began to gather again.

Shutting his ears to the clamour, Axel looked around at the villa, counting the six columns in the portico, then gazed out across the lawn at the silver disc of the lake, its bowl reflecting the last evening light, and at the shadows moving between the tall trees, lengthening across the crisp turf. He lingered over the bridge where he and his wife had stood arm in arm for so many summers –

'*Axel!*'

The tumult outside roared into the air, a thousand voices bellowed only twenty or thirty yards away. A stone flew over the wall and landed among the time flowers, snapping several of the brittle stems. The Countess ran towards him as a further barrage rattled along the wall. Then a heavy tile whirled through the air over their heads and crashed into one of the conservatory windows.

'Axel!' He put his arms around her, straightening his silk cravat when her shoulders brushed it between his lapels.

'Quickly, my dear, the last flower!' He led her down the steps and through the garden. Taking the stem between her jewelled fingers, she snapped it cleanly, then cradled it within her palms.

For a moment the tumult lessened slightly and Axel collected himself. In the vivid light sparkling from the flower he saw his wife's white, frightened eyes. 'Hold it as long as you can, my dear, until the last grain dies.'

Together they stood on the terrace, the Countess clasping the brilliant dying jewel, the air closing in upon them as the voices outside mounted again. The mob was battering at the heavy iron gates, and the whole villa shook with the impact.

While the final glimmer of light sped away, the Countess raised her palms to the air, as if releasing an invisible bird, then in a final access of courage put her hands in her husband's, her smile as radiant as the vanished flower.

'Oh, Axel!' she cried.

Like a sword, the darkness swooped down across them.

Heaving and swearing, the outer edges of the mob reached the knee-high remains of the wall enclosing the ruined estate, hauled their carts over it and along the dry ruts of what once had been an ornate drive. The ruin, formerly a spacious villa, barely interrupted the ceaseless tide of humanity. The lake was empty, fallen trees rotting at its bottom, an old bridge rusting into it. Weeds flourished among the long grass in the lawn, over-running the ornamental pathways and carved stone screens.

Much of the terrace had crumbled, and the main section of the mob cut straight across the lawn, by-passing the gutted villa, but one or two of the more curious climbed up and searched among the shell. The doors had rotted from their hinges and the floors had fallen through. In the music-room an ancient harpsichord had been chopped into firewood, but a few keys still lay among the dust. All the books had been toppled from the shelves in the library, the canvases had been slashed, and gilt frames littered the floor.

As the main body of the mob reached the house, it began to cross the wall at all points along its length. Jostled together, the people stumbled into the dry lake, swarmed over the terrace and pressed through the house towards the open doors on the north side.

One area alone withstood the endless wave. Just below the terrace, between the wrecked balcony and the wall, was a dense, six-foot-high growth of heavy thorn-bushes. The barbed foliage formed an impenetrable mass, and the people passing stepped around it carefully, noticing the belladonna entwined among branches. Most of them were too busy finding their footing among the upturned flagstones to look up into the centre of the thornbushes, where two stone statues stood side by side, gazing out over the grounds from their protected vantage point. The larger of the figures was the effigy of a bearded man in a high-collared jacket, a cane under one arm. Beside him was a woman in an elaborate full-skirted dress, her slim, serene face unmarked by the wind and rain. In her left hand she lightly clasped a single rose, the delicately formed petals so thin as to be almost transparent.

As the sun died away behind the house a single ray of light glanced through a shattered cornice and struck the rose, reflected off the whorl of petals on to the statues, lighting up the grey stone so that for a fleeting moment it was indistinguishable from the long-vanished flesh of the statues' originals.

The Fog Horn

Ray Bradbury

Out there in the cold water, far from land, we waited every night for the coming of the fog, and it came, and we oiled the brass machinery and lit the fog light up in the stone tower. Feeling like two birds in the grey sky, McDunn and I sent the light touching out, red, then white, then red again, to eye the lonely ships. And if they did not see our light, then there was always our Voice, the great deep cry of our Fog Horn shuddering through the rags of mist to startle the gulls away like decks of scattered cards and make the waves turn high and foam.

'It's a lonely life, but you're used to it now, aren't you?' asked McDunn.

'Yes,' I said. 'You're a good talker, thank the Lord.'

'Well, it's your turn on land tomorrow,' he said, smiling, 'to dance with the ladies and drink gin.'

'What do you think, McDunn, when I leave you out here alone?'

'On the mysteries of the sea.' McDunn lit his pipe. It was a quarter past seven of a cold November evening, the heat on, the light switching its tail in two hundred directions, the Fog Horn bumbling in the high throat of the tower. There wasn't a town for a hundred miles down the coast, just a road which came lonely through dead country to the sea, with few cars on it, a stretch of two miles of cold water out to our rock, and rare few ships.

'The mysteries of the sea,' said McDunn thoughtfully. 'You know, the ocean's the biggest damned snowflake ever? It rolls and swells a thousand shapes and colours, no two alike. Strange. One night, years ago, I was here alone, when all of the fish of the sea surfaced out there. Something made them swim in and lie in the bay, sort of trembling and staring up at the tower light going red, white, red, white across them so I could see their funny eyes. I turned cold. They were like a peacock's tail, moving out there until midnight. Then, without so much as a sound, they slipped away, the million of them was gone. I kind of think maybe, in some sort of way, they came all those miles to worship. Strange. But think how the tower must look to them, standing seventy feet above the water, the God-light flashing out from it, and the tower declaring itself with a monster voice. They never came back, those fish, but don't you think for a while they thought they were in the Presence?'

I shivered. I looked out at the long grey lawn of the sea stretching away into nothing and nowhere.

'Oh, the sea's full.' McDunn puffed his pipe nervously, blinking. He had been nervous all day and hadn't said why. 'For all our engines and so-called submarines, it'll be ten thousand centuries before we set foot on the real bottom of the sunken lands, in the fairy kingdoms there, and know *real* terror. Think of it, it's still the year 300,000 Before Christ down under there. While we've paraded around with trumpets, lopping off each other's countries and heads, they have been living beneath the sea twelve miles deep and cold in a time as old as the beard of a comet.'

'Yes, it's an old world.'

'Come on. I got something special I been saving up to tell you.'

We ascended the eighty steps, talking and taking our time. At the top, McDunn switched off the room lights so there'd be no reflection in the plate glass. The great eye of the light was humming, turning easily in its oiled socket. The Fog Horn was blowing steadily, once every fifteen seconds.

'Sounds like an animal, don't it?' McDunn nodded to himself. 'A big lonely animal crying in the night. Sitting here on the edge of ten billion years calling out to the Deeps, I'm here, I'm here, I'm here. And the Deeps *do* answer, yes, they do. You been here now for three months, Johnny, so I better prepare you. About this time of year,' he said, studying the murk and fog, 'something comes to visit the lighthouse.'

'The swarms of fish like you said?'

'No, this is something else. I've put off telling you because you might think I'm daft. But tonight's the latest I can put it off, for if my calendar's marked right from last year, tonight's the night it comes. I won't go into detail, you'll have to see it yourself. Just sit down there. If you want, tomorrow you can pack your duffel and take the motorboat in to land and get your car parked there at the dinghy pier on the cape and drive on back to some little inland town and keep your lights burning nights, I won't question or blame you. It's happened three years now, and this is the only time anyone's been here with me to verify it. You wait and watch.'

Half an hour passed with only a few whispers between us. When we grew tired waiting, McDunn began describing some of his ideas to me. He had some theories about the Fog Horn itself.

'One day many years ago a man walked along and stood in the sound of the ocean on a cold sunless shore and said, "We need a voice to call across the water, to warn ships; I'll make one. I'll make a voice like all of time and all of the fog that ever was; I'll make a voice that is like an empty bed beside you all night long, and like an empty house when you open the door, and like trees in autumn with no leaves. A sound like the birds flying south, crying, and a sound like November wind and the sea on the hard, cold shore. I'll make a sound that's so alone that no one can miss it, that whoever hears it will weep in their souls, and hearths will seem warmer, and being inside will seem better to all who hear it in the distant towns. I'll make a sound and an apparatus and they'll call it a Fog Horn and whoever hears it will know the sadness of eternity and the briefness of life." '

The Fog Horn blew.

'I made up that story,' said McDunn quietly, 'to try to explain why this thing keeps coming back to the lighthouse every year. The Fog Horn calls it, I think, and it comes . . . '

'But – ' I said.

'Sssst!' said McDunn. 'There!' He nodded out to the Deeps.

Something was swimming towards the lighthouse tower.

It was a cold night, as I have said; the high tower was cold, the light coming and going, and the Fog Horn calling and calling through the ravelling mist. You couldn't see far and you couldn't see plain, but there was the deep sea moving on its way about the night earth, flat and quiet, the colour of grey mud, and here were the two of us alone in the high tower, and there, far out at first, was a ripple, followed by a wave, a rising, a bubble, a bit of froth. And then, from the surface of the cold sea came a head, a large head, dark-coloured, with immense eyes, and then a neck. And then – not a body – but more neck and more! The head rose a full forty feet above the water on a slender and beautiful dark neck. Only then did the body, like a little island of black coral and shells and crayfish, drip up from the subterranean. There was a flicker of tail. In all, from head to tip of tail, I estimated the monster at ninety or a hundred feet.

I don't know what I said. I said something.

'Steady, boy, steady,' whispered McDunn.

'It's impossible!' I said.

'No, Johnny, *we're* impossible. *It's* like it always was ten million years ago. *It* hasn't changed. It's *us* and the land that've changed, bcome impossible. *Us!*'

It swam slowly and with a great dark majesty out in the icy waters, far away. The fog came and went about it, momentarily erasing its shape. One of the monster eyes caught and held and flashed back our immense light, red, white, red, white, like a disc held high and sending a message in primeval code. It was as silent as the fog through which it swam.

'It's a dinosaur of some sort!' I crouched down, holding to the stair rail.

'Yes, one of the tribe.'

'But they died out!'

'No, only hid away in the Deeps. Deep, deep down in the deepest Deeps. Isn't *that* a word now, Johnny, a real world, it says so much: the Deeps. There's all the coldness and darkness and deepness in the world in a word like that.'

'What'll we do?'

'Do? We got our job, we can't leave. Besides, we're safer here than in any boat trying to get to land. That thing's as big as a destroyer and almost as swift.'

'But here, why does it come *here*?'

The next moment I had my answer.

The Fog Horn blew.

And the monster answered.

A cry came across a million years of water and mist. A cry so anguished and alone that it shuddered in my head and my body. The monster cried out at the tower. The Fog Horn blew. The monster roared again. The Fog Horn blew. The monster opened its great toothed mouth and the sound that came from it was the sound of the Fog Horn itself. Lonely and vast and far away. The sound of isolation, a viewless sea, a cold night, apartness. That was the sound.

'Now,' whispered McDunn, 'do you know why it comes here?'

I nodded.

'All year long, Johnny, that poor monster there lying far out, a thousand miles at sea, and twenty miles deep maybe, biding it's time, perhaps it's a million years old, this one creature. Think of it, waiting a million years; could *you* wait that long? Maybe it's the last of its kind. I sort of think that's true. Anyway, here come men on land and build this lighthouse, five years ago. And set up their Fog Horn and sound it and sound it, out towards the place where you bury yourself in sleep and sea memories of a world where there were thousands like yourself, but now you're alone, all alone in a world not made for you, a world where you have to hide.

'But the sound of the Fog Horn comes and goes, comes and goes, and you stir from the muddy bottom of the Deeps, and your eyes open like the lenses of two-foot cameras and you move, slow, slow, for you have the ocean sea on your shoulders, heavy. But that Fog Horn comes through a thousand miles of water, faint and familiar, and the furnace in your belly stokes up, and you begin to rise, slow, slow. You feed yourself on great slakes of cod and minnow, on rivers of jellyfish, and you rise slow through the autumn months, through September when the fogs started, through October with more fog and the horn still calling you on, and then, late in November, after pressurizing yourself day by day, a few feet higher every hour, you are near the surface and still alive. You've got to go slow; if you surfaced all at once you'd explode. So it takes you all of three months to surface, and then a number of days to swim through the cold waters to the lighthouse. And there you are, out there, in the night, Johnny, the biggest damn monster in creation. And here's the lighthouse calling to you, with a long neck like your neck sticking way up out of the water, and a body like your body, and, most important of all, a voice like your voice. Do you understand now, Johnny, do you understand?'

The Fog Horn blew.

The monster answered.

I saw it all, I knew it all – the million years of waiting alone, for someone to come back who never came back. The million years of isolation at the bottom of the sea, the insanity of time there, while the skies cleared of reptile-birds, the swamps dried on the continental lands, the sloths and sabretooths had their day and sank in tar pits, and men ran like white ants upon the hills.

The Fog Horn blew.

'Last year,' said McDunn, 'that creature swam round and round, round and round, all night. Not coming too near, puzzled, I'd say. Afraid, maybe. And a bit angry after coming all this way. But the next day, unexpectedly, the fog lifted, the sun came out fresh, the sky was as blue as a painting. And the monster swam off away from the heat and the silence and didn't come back. I suppose it's been brooding on it for a year now, thinking it over from every which way.'

The monster was only a hundred yards off now, it and the Fog Horn crying at each other. As the lights hid them, the monster's eyes were fire and ice, fire and ice.

'That's life for you,' said McDunn. 'Someone always waiting for someone who never comes home. Always someone loving some thing more than that thing loves them. And after a while you want to destroy whatever that thing is, so it can't hurt you no more.'

The Fog Horn blew.

'Let's see what happens,' said McDunn.

He switched the Fog Horn off.

The ensuing minute of silence was so intense that we could hear our hearts pounding in the glassed area of the tower, could hear the slow greased turn of the light.

The monster stopped and froze. Its great lantern eyes blinked. Its mouth gaped. It gave a sort of rumble, like a volcano. It twitched its head this way and that, as if to seek the sounds now dwindled off into the fog. It peered at the lighthouse. It rumbled again. Then its eyes caught fire. It reared up, threshed the water, and rushed at the tower, its eyes filled with angry torment.

'McDunn!' I cried. 'Switch on the horn!'

McDunn fumbled with the switch. But even as he flicked it on, the monster was rearing up. I had a glimpse of its gigantic paws, fishskin flittering in webs between the fingerlike projections, clawing at the tower. The huge eye on the right side of its anguished head glittered before me like a cauldron into which I might drop, screaming. The tower shook. The Fog Horn cried; the monster cried. It seized the tower and gnashed the glass, which shattered in upon us.

McDunn seized my arm. 'Downstairs!'

The tower rocked, trembled, and started to give. The Fog Horn and the monster roared. We stumbled and half fell down the stairs. 'Quick!'

We reached the bottom as the tower buckled down towards us. We ducked under the stairs into the small stone cellar. There were a thousand concussions as the rocks rained down; the Fog Horn stopped abruptly. The monster crashed upon the tower. The tower fell. We knelt together, McDunn and I, holding tight, while our world exploded.

Then it was over, and there was nothing but darkness and the wash of the sea on the raw stones.

That and the other sound.

'Listen,' said McDunn quietly. 'Listen.'

We waited a moment. And then I began to hear it. First a great vacuumed sucking of air, and then the lament, the bewilderment, the loneliness of the great monster, folded over and upon us, so that the sickening reek of its body filled the air, a stone's thickness away from our cellar. The monster gasped and cried. The tower was gone. The light was gone. The thing that had called to it across a million years was gone. And the monster was opening its mouth and sending out great sounds. The sounds of a Fog Horn, again and again. And ships far at sea, not finding the light, not seeing anything, but passing and hearing late that night, must've thought: There it is, the lonely sound, the Lonesome Bay horn. All's well. We've rounded the cape.

And so it went for the rest of that night.

The sun was hot and yellow the next afternoon when the rescuers came out to dig us from our stoned-under cellar.

'It fell apart, is all,' said Mr McDunn gravely. 'We had a few bad knocks from the waves and it just crumbled.' He pinched my arm.

There was nothing to see. The ocean was calm, the sky blue. The only thing was a great algaic stink from the green matter that covered the fallen tower stones and the shore rocks. Flies buzzed about. The ocean washed empty on the shore.

The next year they built a new lighthouse, but by that time I had a job in the little town and a wife and a good small warm house that glowed yellow on autumn nights, the doors locked, the chimney puffing smoke. As for McDunn, he was master of the new lighthouse, built to his own specifications, out of steel-reinforced concrete. 'Just in case,' he said.

The new lighthouse was ready in November. I drove down alone one evening late and parked my car and looked across the grey waters and listened to the new horn sounding, once, twice, three, four times a minute far out there, by itself.

The monster?

It never came back.

'It's gone away,' said McDunn. 'It's gone back to the Deeps.

It's learned you can't love anything too much in this world. It's gone into the deepest Deeps to wait another million years. Ah, the poor thing! Waiting out there, and waiting out there, while man comes and goes on this pitiful little planet. Waiting and waiting.'

I sat in my car, listening. I couldn't see the lighthouse or the light standing out in Lonesome Bay. I could only hear the Horn, the Horn, the Horn. It sounded like the monster calling.

I sat there wishing there was something I could say.

The Wife's Story

Ursula Le Guin

He was a good husband, a good father. I don't understand it. I don't believe in it. I don't believe that it happened. I saw it happen but it isn't true. It can't be. He was always gentle. If you'd have seen him playing with the children, anybody who saw him with the children would have known that there wasn't any bad in him, not one mean bone. When I first met him he was still living with his mother, over near Spring Lake, and I used to see them together, the mother and the sons, and think that any young fellow that was that nice with his family must be one worth knowing. Then one time when I was walking in the woods I met him by himself coming back from a hunting trip. He hadn't got any game at all, not so much as a field mouse, but he wasn't cast down about it. He was just larking along enjoying the morning air. That's one of the things I first loved about him. He didn't take things hard, he didn't grouch and whine when things didn't go his way. So we got to talking that day. And I guess things moved right along after that, because pretty soon he was over here pretty near all the time. And my sister said – see, my parents had moved out the year before and gone south, leaving us the place – my sister said, kind of teasing but serious, 'Well! If he's going to be here every day and half the night, I guess there isn't room for me!' And she moved out – just down the way. We've always been real close, her and me. That's the sort of thing doesn't ever change. I couldn't ever have got through this bad time without my sis.

Well, so he come to live here. And all I can say is, it was the happy year of my life. He was just purely good to me. A hard worker and never lazy, and so big and fine-looking. Everybody looked up to him, you know, young as he was. Lodge Meeting nights, more and more often they had him to lead the singing.

He had such a beautiful voice, and he'd lead off strong, and the others following and joining in, high voices and low. It brings the shivers on me now to think of it, hearing it, nights when I'd stayed home from meeting when the children was babies – the singing coming up through the trees there, and the moonlight, summer nights, the full moon shining. I'll never hear anything so beautiful. I'll never know a joy like that again.

It was the moon, that's what they say. It's the moon's fault, and the blood. It was in his father's blood. I never knew his father, and now I wonder what become of him. He was from up Whitewater way, and had no kin around here. I always thought he went back there, but now I don't know. There was some talk about him, tales that come out after what happened to my husband. It's something runs in the blood, they say, and it may never come out, but if it does, it's the change of the moon that does it. Always it happens in the dark of the moon. When everybody's home and asleep. Something comes over the one that's got the curse in his blood, they say, and he gets up because he can't sleep and goes out into the glaring sun, and goes off all alone – drawn to find those like him.

And it may be so, because my husband would do that. I'd half rouse and say, 'Where are you going to?' and he'd say, 'Oh, hunting, be back this evening,' and it wasn't like him, even his voice was different. But I'd be so sleepy, and not wanting to wake the kids, and he was so good and responsible, it was no call of mine to go asking, 'Why?' and 'Where?' and all like that.

So it happened that way maybe three times or four. He'd come back late, and worn out, and pretty near cross for one so sweet tempered – not wanting to talk about it. I figured everybody got to bust out now and then, and nagging never helped anything. But it did begin to worry me. Not so much that he went, but that he come back so tired and strange. Even, he smelled strange. It made my hair stand up on end. I could not endure it and I said, 'What is that – those smells on you? All over you!' And he said, 'I don't know,' real short, and made like he was sleeping. But he went down when he thought I wasn't noticing, and washed and washed himself. But those smells stayed in his hair, and in our bed, for days.

And then the awful thing. I don't find it easy to tell about this. I want to cry when I have to bring it to my mind. Our youngest, the little one, my baby, she turned from her father. Just overnight. He come in and she got scared-looking, stiff, with her eyes wide, and then she began to cry and try to hide behind me. She didn't yet talk plain but she was saying over and over, 'Make it go away! Make it go away!'

The look in his eyes, just for one moment, when he heard that. That's what I don't want ever to remember. That's what I can't forget. The look in his eyes looking at his own child.

I said to the child, 'Shame on you, what's got into you!' – scolding, but keeping her right up close to me at the same time, because I was frightened too. Frightened to shaking.

He looked away then and said something like. 'Guess she just waked up dreaming,' and passed it off that way. Or tried to. And so did I. And I got real mad with my baby when she kept on acting crazy scared of her own dad. But she couldn't help it and I couldn't change it.

He kept away that whole day. Because he knew, I guess. It was just beginning dark of the moon.

It was hot and close inside, and dark, and we'd all been asleep some while, when something woke me up. He wasn't there beside me. I heard a little stir in the passage, when I listened. So I got up, because I could bear it no longer. I went out into the passage, and it was light there, hard sunlight coming in from the door. And I saw him standing just outside, in the tall grass by the entrance. His head was hanging. Presently he sat down, like he felt weary, and looked down at his feet. I held still, inside and watched – I don't know what for.

And I saw what he saw. I saw the changing. In his feet, it was, first. They got long, each foot got longer, stretching out, the toes stretching out and the foot getting long, and fleshy, and white. And no hair on them.

The hair begun to come away all over his body. It was like his hair fried away in the sunlight and was gone. He was white all over, then, like a worm's skin. And he turned his face. It was changing while I looked. It got flatter and flatter, the mouth flat and wide, and the teeth grinning flat and dull, and the nose just a knob of flesh with nostril holes, and the ears gone, and the eyes gone blue – blue, with white rims around the blue – staring at me out of that flat, soft, white face.

He stood up then on two legs.

I saw him, I had to see him, my own dear love, turned into the hateful one.

I couldn't move, but as I crouched there in the passage staring out into the day I was trembling and shaking with a growl that burst out into a crazy, awful howling. A grief howl and a terror howl and a calling howl. And the others heard it, even sleeping, and woke up.

It stared and peered, that thing my husband had turned into, and shoved its face up to the entrance of our house. I was still bound by mortal fear, but behind me the children had waked up, and the baby was whimpering. The mother anger come into me then, and I snarled and crept forward.

The man thing looked around. It had no gun, like the ones from the man places do. But it picked up a heavy fallen tree branch in its long white foot, and shoved the end of that down into our house, at me. I snapped the end of it in my teeth and started to force my way out, because I knew the man would kill our children if it could. But my sister was already coming. I saw her running at the man with her head low and her mane high and her eyes yellow as the winter sun. It turned on her and raised up that branch to hit her. But I come out of the doorway, mad with the mother anger, and the others all were coming answering my call, the whole pack gathering, there in that blind glare and heat of the sun at noon.

The man looked round at us and yelled out loud, and brandished the branch it held. Then it broke and ran, heading for the cleared fields and plowlands, down the mountainside. It ran, on two legs, leaping and weaving, and we followed it.

I was last, because love still bound the anger and the fear in me. I was running when I saw them pull it down. My sister's teeth were in its throat. I got there and it was dead. The others were drawing back from the kill, because of the taste of the blood, and the smell. The younger ones were cowering and some crying, and my sister rubbed her mouth against her forelegs over and over to get rid of the taste. I went up close because I thoughif the thing was dead the spell, the curse must be done, and my husband would come back – alive, or even dead, if I could only see him, my true love, in his true form, beautiful. But only the dead man lay there white and bloody. We drew back and back from it, and turned and ran, back up into the hills, back to the woods of the shadows and the twilight and the blessed dark.

Sing a Last Song of Valdese

Karl Edward Wagner

1 The Girl Beneath the Oak

'Reverence! Hold up a moment!'

The burly priest drew rein in a swirl of autumn leaves. Calloused fingers touched the plain hilt of the sword strapped to his saddle as his cowled head bent in the direction of her call.

Raven-black hair twining in the autumn wind, the girl stepped out from the gnarled oaks that shouldered the mountain trail. Bright black eyes smiled up at him from her wide-browed, strong-boned face. Her mouth was wide as well, and smiled.

'You ride fast this evening, reverence.'

'Because the shadows grow deeper, and I have a good way to ride to reach the inn ahead.' His voice was impatient.

'There's an inn not more than a mile from here.' She swayed closer, and he saw her full figure swelled against her long-skirted dress.

The priest followed the gesture. Just ahead the trail forked, the left winding alongside the mountain river, the right cutting along the base of the ridge. While the river road bore signs of regular travel, the other trail showed an aspect of disuse. Towards this the girl was pointing.

'That trail leads toward Rader,' he told her, shifting in his saddle. 'My business is in Carrasahl.'

'Besides,' he added, 'I was told the inn near the fork of the road had long been abandoned. Few have cause to travel to Rader since the wool fair was shifted south to Enseljos.'

'The old inn has lately been reopened.'

'That may be. But my path lies to Carrasahl.'

She pouted. 'I was hoping you might carry me with you to the inn yonder.'

'Climb up and I'll take you to the inn on the Carrasahl road.'

'But my path lies to Rader.'

The priest shrugged thick shoulders, beneath his cassock. 'Then you'd best be going.'

'But reverence,' her voice pleaded. 'It will be dark long before I reach the inn, and I'm afraid to walk this trail at night. Won't you take me there on your horse? It won't take you far from your way, and you can lodge the night there just as well.'

Shadows were lengthening, merging into dusk along the foot of the ridges. The declining sun shed only a dusty rubrous haze across the hilltops, highlighting tall hardwoods already fired by autumn's touch. Streaked with mist, the valleys beyond were swallowed in twilight.

Night was fast overtaking him, the rider saw. He recalled the warnings of villagers miles behind, who for his blessing had given him food and sour wine. They had answered his questions concerning the road ahead, then warned him to keep to the trail if night caught him and on no account make camp by himself. The priest had not been certain whether they warned him of robbers or some darker threat.

His horse stamped impatiently.

'I could make it worth your while to ride out of your way.'

About to ride off, he glanced back down at her. Her smile was impish. Hidden by the cowl, his face could not be read.

She touched the ties of her embroidered bodice. 'I would see that you had a most pleasant stay at Vald's Cove Inn, reverence.' There was witchery in her voice. The bodice loosened, parted across her breasts.

'Though I can't see your face, I can see there's a man beneath that priest's cassock. Would you like to enjoy a mountain flower tonight? You'll remember her sweetness when you grow old in some musty temple.' . . .

Whatever his interest in her, the priest carried gold beneath his robe. The girl's eagerness to draw him onto a little-frequented trail aroused deep suspicion.

'The lure of wanton flesh is nothing to a priest of Thoem,' he intoned.

. . . She spat, and lunged with a shrill scream for his horse's face. Sharp claws raked blood across his nose.

Already nervous, the horse screamed and reared. Caught by surprise, the priest lost his stirrups. Cassock flapping about his limbs, he scrambled for balance, then was thrown from the terrified mount. He fell heavily, somehow landing half on his feet, and cursed as his ankle turned under him.

The rearing horse bolted down the trail, took the right fork toward Rader, and disappeared. With mocking laughter, the girl ran after.

Limping badly, the priest stumbled after her, cursing with blasphemous invective. But the darkness quickly swallowed the flash of her white legs, though her laughter taunted him invisibly still.

2 The Inn by the Side of the Road

The lights of the inn were smoky yellow through the thick, leaded panes. The night winds caught the smoke and smell of horses, drove it down the road to Rader, so that the priest came upon the inn all at once.

He noted the many horses tethered in the outlying stables. There were a number of travellers at the inn tonight, and it seemed less likely that the girl meant to lead him into a trap. Or had her confederates lain in wait along the trail, probably they were content to steal his horse and gear. The priest swore angrily, decided he had been too suspicious.

His ankle stabbed with pain, but at least it bore his weight. His boots had probably prevented worse injury. He damned the voluminous grey cassock as it flapped about his trousered legs. It was slitted front and back from ankle to midthigh, and while that enabled him to straddle a horse, he blamed the clumsy garment for his fall.

The two-storey square log structure was a welcome sight. The autumn night grew chill; mist flowed like waves across the ridges. A night spent in the open would be uncomfortable at best. Worse, he had been warned of danger, and his sword was strapped to his saddle somewhere in the darkened hills.

A sign hung over the door: Vald's Cove Inn. The carving seemed of recent work, the priest noted as he climbed up to the door. The latch was not out, though the hour was not late. Hearing voices within, he knocked loudly.

He was about to knock a third time, when the door was opened. Light and voices and the smell of warmth spilled out into the night.

A narrow, beardless face frowned out at him from the half-open doorway. 'Who . . . what do you want . . . reverence?' His voice was thin and nervous, and he spoke in a half-whisper.

'Food and lodging,' the priest rumbled impatiently. 'This *is* an inn, I believe.'

'I'm sorry. There's no more room. You'll have to go elsewhere.' He made to close the door.

The priest's huge fist checked him. 'Are you a fool?' Where is the innkeeper?' he demanded, suspicious at the man's show of anxious confusion.

'I'm master here,' the other snapped in annoyance. 'I'm sorry, reverence. I've no more room, and you'll have to – '

'Look, damn you!' The priest's bulk shouldered onto the threshold. 'My horse threw me, and I've hobbled for miles already to get here. Now I'll have food and lodging if it's no more than floor space near the fire!'

The skeletal innkeeper did not quail before the bigger man. His narrow jaw clamped in anger; he clenched his black-gloved hands.

'What is this, man?' demanded a voice from within. 'Do I hear you denying lodging to a brother servant of Thoem! What manner of innkeeper are you?'

The innkeeper started, then cringed effusively. 'Forgive me, eminence. I only meant that my accommodations were not sufficient for one of his reverence's – '

'Let him in, you idiot! Turn away a priest of Thoem, would you! I see it's true how sadly you mountain folk have fallen in your respect for the true god! Let him in, do you hear?'

The priest pushed past the suddenly solicitous innkeeper. 'Thank you, eminence. The manners of these folk are pitiable.'

There were several people in the common room of the inn. Seated alone at one of several tables was a tall, thin man whose scarlet cassock identified him as an abbot in the priesthood of Thoem. Like the priest, his face was hidden by the cowled garment. He waved to the other man with a finely groomed, blue-veined hand.

'Come join me by the fire and have some wine,' he invited. 'I see you're limping somewhat. Did I hear you say your horse threw you? That's bad luck. Our host must send his servants out to find it. Are you badly hurt?'

'Thoem saved me from serious harm, eminence, though I'd rather not walk another mile on it tonight.'

'I'm certain. More wine, innkeeper! And hurry with that roast! Would you starve your guests? Sit down here, please. Have we met? I am Passlo, on my way in the service of Thoem to take charge of the abbey at Rader.'

'A pleasure to meet you, Eminent Passlo.' The priest touched hands as he seated himself. 'I am Callistratis, journeying in the service of Thoem to Carrasahl. I've heard the abbey at Rader has fallen to the Dualists in these evil times.'

The abbot scowled. 'Certain rumors have reached us in the South. Word that there are certain rebel priests in the northern provinces who would contend that Thoem and Vaul are but dual expressions of the same deity. No doubt these heretics consider it prudent to align themselves with the god of these northern barbarians, now that the empire drifts into civil war.'

The priest poured wine and drank hunched forward so that his lips were hidden in the shadow of his cowl. 'I have heard such attempts to vindicate the Dualist heresy. It may be that our errands are the same, Eminent Passlo.'

'Well, Revered Callistratis, that doesn't surprise me. I'd

sensed immediately that there was a presence about you that argued for more than the simple priest. But I'll not intrude further on one whose mission requires that he travel incognito. But tell me, how would you deal with the Dualists?'

'By the prescribed formula for any heresy. They should all suffer impalement, their bodies left for night beasts and carrion birds.'

The abbot clapped him on the shoulder. 'Splendid, Revered Callistratis! We are of one accord! It pleases me to know that those who believe unswervingly in Thoem's sacred precepts have not all passed from the priesthood! I foresee a pleasant evening of theological discussion.'

'Come, revered gentlemen, don't judge too harshly. After all, there is precedent for Dualism in the history of your priesthood.'

A short, stocky gentleman with a fine grey beard looked gravely at the priest. He straightened from the fire where he had stooped to light his pipe. A silver medallion embossed with a university seal depended from a chain about his thick neck.

'Precedent?' the abbot snapped.

The short man nodded through a puff of smoke. 'Yes, I refer to the dogma formalized under the reign of King Halbros I that Thro'ellet and Tloluvin are but dual identities of the evil principle. No one in the days of the monarchy considered such doctrine heretical, although ancient beliefs plainly ascribe separate identities to those demonlords.

The abbot paused to consider. 'An interesting point,' he conceded grudgingly, 'although the manifold embodiments of evil are certainly acknowledged by our doctrine. Nonetheless, your argument does not hold in this instance, for there is but one true cosmic principle of good, whom true believers worship as Thoem. May I inquire, sir . . . ?

The grey-bearded gentleman blew smoke in a flourish. 'I am Claesna, of the Imperial University of Chrosanthe. Your proposal of theological debate caught my ear, eminence. The prospect of intelligent discussion promises salvation from what I had previously feared would be a dull evening in a backwoods tavern. May I join you?'

'Claesna?' The abbot's tone was surprise. 'Yes, I've heard a great deal of you, sir. Please join us! Why does a scholar of your high renown pass through these dismal mountains?'

Claesna smiled acknowledgement. 'I'm headed for Rader myself, actually. I've heard of certain inscriptions on what are said to be prehuman ruins near there. If so, I'd like to copy them for study and comparison with others that I've seen.'

'So it's true you plan to supplement Nentali's *Interpretation of Elder Glyphics*?' suggested the grey-cowled priest.

Claesna lifted a bushy eyebrow. '*Supplant*, not *supplement*, Revered Callistratis. Well, I see you are an extraordinarily well-informed man yourself. This *does* promise to be an illuminating evening.'

'Oh, please, learned gentlemen,' mimicked a sneering voice from the corner. 'Don't bore us all to death with such learned discussions.'

'Shut up, Hef!' A gruff voice cut him off. 'You'll find a neater death than boredom when we get to Rader!'

The other made an obscene reply. An open fist slapped on flesh, then sounded the clash of chains, subdued cursing.

'Ranvyas, you son of a pox-eaten whore, you busted that tooth half out of my head. Takes guts for a pissant bounty hunter like you to bust a man all chained up.'

'You had an even chance before the chains went on, Hef,' growled Ranvyas. 'And you won't need that tooth once I get you to Rader.'

'We'll see, Ranvyas. Oh, we'll see, won't we? There was other smart b.....ds all set to count their bounty money, but ain't one of them lived to touch a coin of it.'

Claesna indicated the two men in the near corner. One was a tall, lantern-jawed swordsman with iron-grey hair who wore the green tunic of a ranger. The other, his prisoner, was a wiry man with pinched face and stained yellow beard, whose blue eyes seemed startlingly innocent for one weighed down with wrist and leg irons.

'That's Mad Hef over there, whose black frame ought to be

known even to you, revered sirs. Looks harmless enough, though I doubt all the prayers of your priesthood could cleanse his soul of the deeds he's committed here in the mountains. They were talking about it before you came in. The ranger finally tracked him to the cave where he laired, and if he succeeds where so many other brave men have failed, the public executioner at Rader is due for a strenuous afternoon.

From the rooms above came the echoing moan of a woman in agony.

The priest started from his chair, then halted half-crouched when none of the room's other occupants seemed to pay heed.

Again the cry of pain ripped through the panelled hallway above, down the narrow log stairway. A door slammed at the foot of the stairs, muffled the outcry.

Two other travellers exchanged glances. One, grotesquely fat, shrugged and continued to devour an apple pastry. His smaller companion shuddered and buried his chinless face in his hands.

'Pray Thoem, make her stop!' he moaned.

The fat man wiped his slobbery lips and reached for another pastry. 'Drink more wine, Dordron. Good for the nerves.'

Passlo's hand pulled at the priest's arm. 'Don't be alarmed, Revered Callistratis. The merchant's young wife is giving birth upstairs. No one thought to mention it. As you see, the father is untroubled. Only his brother seems a bit shaken.'

'The fat blob is a half-wit!' sneered Claesna. 'I judge his mind is rotten with pox. I pity his wife, poor child. If our host hadn't sent a serving girl to stay with her, these swine would certainly have left her to labour alone.'

'The mystery of birth,' quoted the abbot, 'where pain is joyful duty.'

Now the innkeeper moved among them, setting before each guest a wooden trencher and a loaf of black bread. Behind him walked a swarthy, bristle-bearded dwarf, the first servant the priest had noted in the inn. His squat, powerful arms carried a great platter of roast meat, which he presented to each guest that he might serve himself as he desired. The fat merchant growled impatiently when the dwarf halted first before the abbot and his two table companions.

'Please Jarcos!' his brother begged. 'Don't offend these revered sirs!'

Hef giggled. 'Don't eat it all now! Save a nice hefty bone for poor toothless Hef!'

From overhead the screams, distant through the thick boards, sounded now at closer intervals.

The innkeeper smiled nervously and wrung his black-gloved hands. 'I'll bring out more wine, Bodger,' he told the dwarf. 'Bring out your mandolin and play for them.'

The dwarf grinned and scuttled into the back rooms. He cavorted out again in a moment, wearing a flop-brim hat with a feather and carrying a black-stained mandolin. His strangely pointed fingers struck the strings like dagger tips, and he began to caper about the room, singing comic ballads in a bullfrog voice.

The moans from upstairs continued monotonously, and soon the travellers forgot to listen to them, or to notice when they ceased.

3 'Do You Know the Song of Valdese?'

'Then, just as the hunter spun around at the sound, the werewolf leaped down from the roof of his cabin! He clawed for the silver dagger at his belt, but the sheath was empty! Too late he remembered the old man's warning! And as he died, he saw that the beast at his throat had the sun-coloured eyes of his wife!'

Claesna leaned back against his chair and blew smoke at the listeners circled about the fire.

'Bravo!' squealed Jarcos, the fat merchant. 'Oh, that was good! Do you mean that the werewolf was really his wife, then?'

Claesna did not deign to reply, instead nodded acceptance of the others' applause.

The meal was a scattering of picked bones and cheese rinds. The autumn night tightened its chill around the inn, where inside the travellers shared the companionship of wine and a warm fire. The hour grew late, but no one yet sought his bed. Pulling chairs in a rough circle about the glowing hearth, they had listened to the ballads of Bodger the dwarf, and as the night wore on someone had suggested that each tell a story.

'The mountains of Halbrosn seemed haunted with all manner of inhuman fiends,' Dordron remarked with a shiver. 'Jarcos, why did you insist we make this journey to Rader? You know the wool market there has been dead for years.'

'My astrologer agreed this was a wise venture. Let me worry about our business, little brother.' Jarcos contrived to shape his rolls of chins into a resolute expression.

'Not only "inhuman fiends" to watch for,' Ranvyas commented, jerking a gnarled thumb toward his prisoner. 'Up until two days ago there was Mad Hef here. Thoem knows how many poor travellers he's waylaid and murdered. Had a favourite trick of crawling out onto the road all covered with blood and moaning he was one of Mad Hef's victims. Too damn many good-hearted folks left their bones in the rocks for the mice to nest in. And I'd as soon forget if I could some of the things I seen back in that cave where he was laired.'

Hef snickered and shook his chains against the post. 'Got a special niche for your skull there, Ranvyas dear. Old man like you should've brought help along, 'stead of trying to sneak after me all alone. You're just too brave for your – '

Ranvyas raised his fist; Hef broke off in an angry mutter.

'There have been human monsters in these mountains worse than this carrion-eater,' the abbot said.

'Oh? Do you know this region, eminence?' asked the innkeeper, who had joined them at the fire.

'Only from my learning. I dare say that the old provinces of the Halbros kings have figured so prominently in our history and literature that all of us know some tale of their mountains – though we are all strangers here.'

He glanced around at the others. 'Perhaps you observed the stone ruins that crest the ridge along the gap ahead. Quite striking against the sunset, I thought. That was the fortress from which Kane held these mountains in thrall for a hundred years. He ruled the land with a bloody fist, exacted tribute from all who passed through, fought back every expedition led against him. Some say he had made a pact with the forces of evil by which they granted him eternal youth and victory in return for the innocent blood he sacrificed each dark of the moon.

'For a while he aided Halbros-Serrantho in the imperial wars, but even the great emperor sickened of Kane's depravity and finally used the combined armies of the new empire to pull the tyrant's citadel down on his head. They say his evil ghost haunts the ruins to this day.'

'A tale somewhat garbled by popular superstition,' Claesna remarked. 'Actually the legend of Kane has far darker implications. His name, I have observed, reappears in all ages and all lands. The literature of the occult recurrently alludes to him. In fact, there is an ancient compendium of prehuman glyphics that Kane is said to have authored. If it exists, I'd give a fortune to read it.'

'A rather long-lived villain, this Kane,' said Passlo drily.

'Some occult authors contend that Kane was one of the first true men, damned to eternal wandering from some dark act of rebellion against mankind's creator.'

'I doubt Thoem would have damned a blasphemer to immortality,' scoffed the abbot. 'Doubtless his legend appeals to certain evil types who take his name for their own.'

'Then they steal his physical appearance, as well,' Claesna countered. 'Legend describes him as a man of powerful build, seemingly a warrior in his prime years. His hair is red and he is left-handed.'

'So are many others.'

'But his eyes are his mark. The eyes of Kane are blue, and in them glows the mad gaze of a ruthless killer. No man may look into Kane's eyes and not know him.'

Ranvyas started. 'There's talk of an assassin who's behind these murders that are pushing the empire into civil war. Said to be an outlander brought in by Eypurin to remove those who oppose his false claim to the throne. His name is reportedly Kane, and what little is known of him answers to your description. Did this Kane die in the fall of his citadel?'

Passlo looked startled. 'Why, of course . . . I suppose. Yes, he must have. That was centuries ago, man!'

'I had been warned against staying the night in the open,' suggested the priest. 'While nothing definite was said, I can see that these mountains have more sinister legends than the road has turns.'

'That's so, Revered Callistratis,' affirmed the ranger, running a hand over his short-cropped hair. 'You say you lost your horse on the trail? Lucky for you you didn't meet Valdese while you was limping along in the dark.'

'Valdese?'

'A lamia, reverence,' explained the innkeeper. 'A most beautiful spectre, Valdese is – and most malevolent. Legend says she haunts the mountain trails at night. Entices travellers into her arms and leaves them bloodless beneath the moon.'

Suddenly it had grown very quiet. Leaves rustled against the frosted windowpanes.

The innkeeper sensed the unease of his guests. 'Had you not heard that legend, gentlemen? But I forgot – you're strangers here, all of you. Still I thought you must have heard her song. Do you know the Song of Valdese?'

He raised a black-gloved hand. 'Come out, Bodger. Sing Valdese's song for our guests.'

The dwarf scuttled out of the shadow with his mandolin. Bowing to his audience, he began to sing, his voice comic no longer.

In the dark hills of Halbros' land,
There dwelled a lovely maid –
The brightest flower, the rarest jewel,
Shone dull in Valdese's hand.

Her father's inn stood beside the road,
Great was his wealth of gold –
But the choicest treasure of the land,
Was the heart of fair Valdese.

Then came brash suitors to her door,
Six bright and bold young men –
Said they had come to win the hand,
Of the maiden called Valdese.

'Sirs,' she said, 'don't think me cruel,
For I love another youth –
He must be gone for seven long years,
To study in a hidden school.'

And when she told them the suitors laughed,
'Oh, your beauty is not for him –
Choose instead from one of our band,
And not some wizard's fool.'

Then came her lover in a cloak of grey,
Returning from the hidden school –
Said, 'I've been gone these seven long years,
Now I've come for the love of Valdese.'

'Oh no,' swore the suitors in jealousy,
'You'll not steal our prize' –
And with cruel knives they took his life,
And the heart of Valdese after.

Now Valdese lies in the cold, cold ground,
And her spirit haunts these hills –
But her lover was sworn in the Grey Lord's name,
To serve seven times seven years.

'That's terrifying!' breathed Dordron, when the dwarf stopped singing. 'So uncanny an ending, that last verse!'

'Perhaps the last verse hasn't been written,' the innkeeper suggested. 'Bodger, see how things are upstairs. It's grown strangely quiet up there.'

'Well, at least we servants of Thoem have nothing to fear from lamiae!' muttered the abbot stoutly. 'Do we not, Revered Callistratis?'

'To be certain, eminence,' the priest assured him. 'Thoem protects his servant from all creatures of evil.'

Passlo suddenly drew a crystal-hilted dagger from the folds of his cassock. 'And for added protection in these shadow-haunted hills I carry with me this sacred blade. It was shaped from starmetal by priests long dead, and the runes on its blade give it power over evil's foul servants.' He did not add that he had stolen the blade from the abbey vaults.

'Seven years in a hidden school,' mused the priest. 'That can only mean one thing.'

Claesna nodded. 'He was apprenticed to the cult of the Seven Nameless – and sworn to the Grey Lord.'

'Thoem grant that we someday see the extinction of that black cult of devil worshippers!' growled Passlo.

'The cult is far older than your own religion,' Claesna informed him. 'And it isn't devil worship, strictly speaking.'

'Well, they're devils they worship!' Jarcos said shrilly.

'No. The Seven Nameless are elder gods. Or "proto-gods", more accurately, since they exist beyond the ordered universe of good and evil forces. Their realm is one of timeless chaos, a limbo of unformed creation and ultimate dissolution – opposite forces that somehow exist simultaneously.'

Claesna preened his beard. 'Their entire worship is structured on the energy of opposing systems. Little is known of the cult, since its devotees worship in secret. New initiates must study seven years in a "hidden school" to master the secret powers of the cult; then each is sworn to one of the Seven for the space of forty-nine years. The names of the Seven are secret, for should the uninitiate utter them he would evoke the god without having power over him. A rather hideous fate, it's said. Korjonos was sworn to the Grey Lord, who is the most feared of the Seven.'

'Korjonos? Was that the young wizard's name?' the priest inquired.

Claesna bit his pipestem testily. 'Yes, I believe so. After all, the ballad was based on true events. Happened a century ago, I believe.'

'Not at all,' corrected the innkeeper. 'Not quite fifty years ago. And very near here.'

'Indeed?' Dordron's voice was strained.

'In fact, at this very inn.'

The eyes of the travellers bored back into their host's smiling face.

'Why, yes. But I forgot you gentlemen are strangers here. Would you like to know the story behind Valdese's song?'

No one spoke. He went on as if there were no tension in the room.

'Valdese and Korjonos were childhood lovers. She was the daughter of one of the richest men in Halbrosn, while he was the son of a servant at his inn. They were both barely past ten when Korjonos was orphaned. Penniless, he left the inn to study at a hidden school and vowed to return for her in seven years, with the wealth and power that his wisdom would bring him.

'Valdese waited for him. But there were others. Six coarse young louts from the settlements close by. They lusted for her beauty, and more for the gold she would inherit. Valdese would not have them, but they argued and waited, for the time was near when Korjonos had promised to return.

'And after seven years he did return. To their brutish anger, Valdese's love for the young wizard had not diminished with time. They were married that night at her father's inn.

'But hate was black in the hearts of her rejected suitors, and they drank long into the night.'

A log burst apart in a shower of sparks, cast light over the circle of nervous faces.

'The guests were gone; her father they slew with the few others who were there. They took his gold, and they dragged the lovers from their wedding chamber.

'They hung Korjonos between two trees. Valdese they threw to the ground.

' "He'll not curse us," said one, and they cut out his tongue.

' "He'll not cast spells against us," said another; and they cut off his hands.

' "Nor seek to follow after us," and they cut off his feet.

'Then they cut away his manhood and told her, "He's not fit to lie with."

'And they cut away his face and told her, "He's not fit to look at."

'But they spared him his eyes so that he might watch what they did to her, and they spared him his ears so he might listen to her screams.

'When they were finished . . . she died. Korjonos they left hanging. Then they divided the gold and fled, each choosing a separate path to follow. And while the infamy of their deed shamed the land, not one of them was ever punished.'

'Korjonos?' asked the priest.

'Did not die. He was sworn to the Grey Lord for seven times seven years, and death could not claim him. His familiar demon cut him down and carried him away. And the rage of the sorcerer waited years upon painful years for fitting vengeance to transpire.'

A chair crashed as Claesna leaped to his feet. 'Gods! Don't you see? It's been near fifty years, and our faces and names were otherwise! But I thought several of your faces seemed familiar to me! Don't deny it! It's no coincidence that all six of us have returned to this inn tonight! Sorcery has drawn us here! But who . . . ?'

The innkeeper smiled in secret mirth as their startled voices shouted in protest. He crossed over to in front of the fire. Still smiling, he peeled off the black gloves.

And they saw what manner of hands were grafted to his wrists. With these hands he dug at the flesh of his face.

The smiling lips peeled away with the rest, and they saw the noseless horror that had been a face, saw the black reptilian tongue that lashed between broken teeth.

They sat frozen in shock. The dwarf entered unnoticed, a tiny corpse in his hairy hands.

'Stillborn, master,' he snickered, holding by its heels the blue-skinned infant. 'Strangled by her cord, and the mother died giving forth.' He stepped into the centre of their circle.

Then the chill of the autumn night bore down upon them, a chill greater than that of any natural darkness.

'Seven years time seven,' hissed Korjonos. 'So long have I plotted for this. I've shaped your lives from the day of your crime, let you fatten like cattle, let you live for the day when you would pay as no man has ever paid!

'Callistratis,' he called aside, 'this isn't for you! I don't know how you came here, but go now if you still can.'

Faces set in fear, they stared at the wizard. Invisible bonds held them in their places about the circle.

Korjonos chanted and gestured. 'Holy man, evil man. Wise man, fool. Brave man, coward. Six corners of the heptagon, and I a dead man who lives, makes the seventh. Contradicting opposites that invoke the chaos lords – and the final paradox is the focus of the spell: an innocent soul who has never lived, a damned soul who can never die!

'Seven times seven years have passed, and when the Grey Lord comes for me, you six shall follow into his realm!'

Suddenly Ranvyas sprang to life. 'The dagger!'

The abbot stared dumbly, then fumbled at his cassock. He seemed to move at a dreamlike pace.

Hissing in rage, Korjonos rushed into the incantation.

Passlo clumsily extended the dagger, but the ranger was faster.

Tearing the dagger from Passlo's trembling fingers, he hurled it at the grinning dwarf.

Bodger shrieked and dropped the stillborn infant. Reeking smoke boiled from his chest where the crystal hilt protruded. He reeled, seemed to sag inward upon himself, like a collapsing coat of mail. Then there was only a charred greasy smear, a pile of filthy clothes – and a hairy spider that scurried away to vanish through a chink in the wall.

'Well done, Ranvyas!' Claesna gasped shakily. 'You've slain his familiar, and the spell is shattered!'

He sneered at the wizard. 'Unless, of course, you've another "damned soul who cannot die" who can complete your incantation.'

Korjonos's bowed shoulders signalled his defeat.

'Let's get out of here!' blubbered Jarcos. His brother was weeping mindlessly.

'Not until we slay the wizard,' growled Ranvyas.

'And set me free,' Hef advised. 'I don't think you'll want me to tell them in Rader about my five old comrades.'

'Thoem! It's cold!' chattered Passlo. 'And what's wrong with the light in here?'

The priest broke into their circle and bent over the pile of seared clothing. They thought he meant to retrieve the enchanted dagger, but when he straightened he held the stillborn child in his left hand.

His cowl fell back. They saw his red hair.

They saw his eyes.

'Kane!' screamed Claesna.

Korjonos shouted out syllables that formed another name.

Hands went for futile swordhilts, but already the room was heavy with the sweet dust stench of ancient decay.

At the doorway behind them the bolt snapped with rust; boards rotted and sagged, crumbled into powdery dissolution. They stared in dread understanding. In the threshold stood a tall figure in a tattered cloak of grey.

Kane turned his face.

And the Grey Lord lifted his mask.

Kane shook the darkness from his mind. He started to come to his feet, then almost fell because he already stood.

He was standing in the gutted interior of a log building. The floor overhead had collapsed, as had the roof, and he could see stars in the night sky. Small trees snagged up through the rotting debris. The inn had been abandoned for many years.

The air was musty with decay. He stumbled for the doorway, thought he heard the snap of dry bones beneath his boots. Outside he breathed raggedly and glanced again at the sky.

The mist crawled in wild patterns across the stars. And Kane saw a wraithlike figure of grey, his cloak flapping in the night winds. Behind him seemed to follow seven more wraiths, dragging their feet as if they would not follow.

Then another phantom. A girl in a long dress, racing after. She caught the seventh follower by the hand. Strained, then drew him away. The Grey Lord and those who must follow vanished into the night skies. The girl and her lover fell back in an embrace – then melted as one into the mist.

Kane's horse was waiting outside the ruined inn. Kane was not surprised, for he had recognized the girl in the mist. His heels touched the horse's flanks, and Kane vanished into the mist as well.

The Test of the Twins

Margaret Weis

The magician and his brother rode through the mists toward the secret place.

'We shouldn't have come,' Caramon muttered. His large, strong hand was on the hilt of his great sword, and his eyes searched every shadow. 'I have been in many dangerous places, but nothing to equal this!'

Raistlin glanced around. He noticed dark, twisted shadows and heard strange sounds.

'They will not bother us, brother,' he said gently. 'We have been invited. They are guardians who keep out the unwanted.' He did, however, draw his red robes closer around his thin body and move to ride nearer Caramon.

'Mages invited us . . . I don't trust 'em.' Caramon scowled.

Raistlin glanced at him. 'Does that include me, dear brother?' he asked softly.

Caramon did not reply.

Although twins, the two brothers could not have been more different. Raistlin, frail and sickly magician and scholar, pondered this difference frequently. They were one whole man split in two: Caramon the body, Raistlin the mind. As such, the two needed and depended on each other far more than other brothers. But, in some ways, it was an unwholesome dependence, for it was as if each was incomplete without the other. At least, this was how it seemed to Raistlin. He bitterly resented whatever gods had played such a trick that cursed him with a weak body when he longed for mastery over others. He was thankful that, at least, he had been granted the skills of a magician. It gave him the power he craved. These skills almost made him the equal of his brother.

Caramon – strong and muscular, a born fighter – always

laughed heartily whenever Raistlin discussed their differences. Caramon enjoyed being his 'little' brother's protector. But, although he was very fond of Raistlin, Caramon pitied his weaker twin. Unfortunately, Caramon had a tendency to express his brotherly concern in unthoughtful ways. He often let his pity show, not realizing it was like a knife twisting in his brother's soul.

Caramon admired his brother's skill as a magician as one admires a festival juggler. He did not treat it seriously or respectfully. Caramon had met neither man nor monster that could not be handled by the sword. Therefore, he could not understand this dangerous trip his brother was undertaking for the sake of his magic.

'It's all parlour tricks, Raist,' Caramon protested. 'Riding into that forsaken land is nothing to risk our lives over.'

Raistlin replied gently – he always spoke gently to Caramon – that he was determined on this course of action for reasons of his own and that Caramon could come if he so chose. Of course, Caramon went. The two had rarely been separated from one another since birth.

The journey was long and hazardous. Caramon's sword was frequently drawn. Raistlin felt his strength ebbing. They were near the end now. Raistlin rode in silence, oppressed with the doubt and fear that shrouded him as it had when he first decided on this course of action. Perhaps Caramon was right, perhaps he was risking their lives needlessly.

It had been three months ago when the Head of the Order arrived at his master's home. Par-Salian had invited Raistlin to visit with him as he dined – much to the master's surprise.

'When do you take the Test, Raistlin?' the old man asked the young conjurer.

'Test?' Raistlin repeated, startled. No need to ask which Test – there was only one.

'He is not ready, Par-Salian,' his master protested. 'He is young – only twenty-one! His spellbook is far from complete – '

'Yes,' Par-Salian interrupted, his eyes narrowing. 'But you believe you are ready, don't you, Raistlin?'

Raistlin had kept his eyes lowered, in the proper show of humility, his hood drawn over his face. Suddenly, he threw back his hood and lifted his head, staring directly, proudly, at Par-Salian. 'I am ready, Great One,' Raistlin spoke coolly.

Par-Salian nodded, his eyes glittering. 'Begin your journey in three months' time,' the old man said, then went back to eating his fish.

Raistlin's master gave him a furious glance, rebuking him for his impudence. Par-Salian did not look at him again. The young conjurer bowed and left without a word.

The servant let him out; however, Raistlin slipped back through the unlocked door, cast a sleep spell upon the servant, and stood, hidden in the alcove, listening to the conversation between his master and Par-Salian.

'The Order has never tested one so young,' the master said. 'And you chose him! Of all my pupils, he is the most unworthy. I simply do not understand.'

'You don't like him, do you?' Par-Salian asked mildly.

'No one does,' the master snapped. 'There is no compassion in him, no humanity. He is greedy and grasping, difficult to trust. Did you know that his nickname among the other students is the Sly One? He absorbs from everyone's soul and gives back nothing of his own. His eyes are mirrors; they reflect all he sees in cold, brittle terms.'

'He is highly intelligent,' Par-Salian suggested.

'Oh, there's no denying that.' The master sniffed. 'He is my best pupil. And he has a natural affinity for magic. Not one of those surface users.'

'Yes,' Par-Salian agreed. 'Raistlin's magic springs from deep within.'

'But it springs from a dark well,' the master said, shaking his head. 'Sometimes I look at him and shudder, seeing the Black Robes fall upon him. That will be his destiny, I fear.'

'I think not,' Par-Salian said thoughtfully. 'There is more to him than you see, though I admit he keeps it well hidden. More to him than he knows himself, I'll wager.'

'Mmmmm,' the master sounded very dubious.

Raistlin smiled to himself, a twisted smile. It came as no surprise to learn his master's true feelings. Raistlin sneered. Who cares? he thought bitterly. As for Par-Salian – Raistlin shrugged it off.

'What of his brother?' Par-Salian asked.

Raistlin, his ear pressed against the door, frowned.

'Ah!' The master became effusive. 'Night and day. Caramon is handsome, honourable, trusting, everyone's friend. Theirs is a strange relationship. I have seen Raistlin watch Caramon with a fierce, burning love in his eyes. And the next instant, I have seen such hatred and jealousy I think the young man could murder his twin without giving it a second thought.' He coughed, apologetically. 'Let me send you Algenon, Great One. He is not as intelligent as Raistlin, but his heart is true and good.'

'Algenon is *too* good,' Par-Salian snorted. 'He has never known torment or suffering or evil. Set him in a cold, biting wind and he will wither like a maiden's first rose. But Raistlin – well, one who constantly battles evil within will not be overly dismayed by evil without.'

Raistlin heard chairs scrape. Par-Salian stood up.

'Let's not argue. I was given a choice to make and I have made it,' Par-Salian said.

'Forgive me, Great One, I did not mean to be contradictory,' the master said stiffly, hurt.

Raistlin heard Par-Salian sigh wearily. 'I should be the one to apologize, old friend,' he said. 'Forgive me. There is trouble coming upon us that the world may not survive. This choice has been a heavy burden upon me. As you know, the Test may well prove fatal to the young man.'

'It has killed others more worthy,' the master murmured.

Their conversation turned to other matters, so Raistlin crept away.

The young mage considered Par-Salian's words many times during the weeks that followed while he prepared for his journey. Sometimes he would hug himself with pride at being chosen by the Great One to take the Test – the greatest honour conferred on a magician. But, at night, the words *may well prove fatal* haunted his dreams.

He thought, as he drew nearer and nearer the Towers, about those who had not survived. Their belongings had been returned to their families, without a single word (other than Par-Salian's regrets). For this reason, many magicians did not take the Test. After all, it gave no additional power. It added no spells to the spellbook. One could practice magic quite well without it, and many did so. But they were not considered 'true' magic-users by their peers, and they knew it. The Test gave a mage an aura that surrounded him. When entering the presence of others, this aura was deeply felt by all and, therefore, commanded respect.

Raistlin hungered for that respect. But did he hunger for it enough to be willing to die trying to obtain it?

'There it is!' Caramon interrupted his thoughts, reining his horse in sharply.

'The fabled Towers of High Sorcery,' Raistlin said, staring in awe.

The three tall stone towers resembled skeletal fingers, clawing out of the grave.

'We could turn back now,' Caramon croaked, his voice breaking.

Raistlin looked at his brother in astonishment. For the first time since he could remember, Raistlin saw fear in Caramon. The young conjurer felt an unusual sensation – a warmth spread over him. He reached out and put a steady hand on his brother's trembling arm. 'Do not be afraid, Caramon,' Raistlin said. 'I am with you.'

Caramon looked at Raistlin, then laughed nervously to himself. He urged his horse forward.

The two entered the Towers. Vast stone walls and darkness swallowed them up, they they heard the voice: 'Approach.'

The two walked ahead. Raistlin walked steadfastly, but Caramon moved warily, his hand on the hilt of his sword. They came to stand before a withered figure sitting in the center of a cold, empty chamber.

'Welcome, Raistlin,' Par-Salian said. 'Do you consider yourself prepared to undergo your final Test?'

'I do, Par-Salian, Greatest of Them All.'

Par-Salian studied the young man before him. The conjurer's pale, thin cheeks were stained with a faint flush, as though fever burned in his blood. 'Who accompanies you?' Par-Salian asked.

'My twin brother, Caramon, Great Mage.' Raistlin's mouth twisted into a snarl. 'As you see, Great One, I am no fighter. My brother came to protect me.'

Par-Salian stared at the brothers, reflecting on the odd humour of the gods. *Twins! This Caramon is huge. Six feet tall, he must weigh over two hundred pounds. His face – face of smiles and boisterous laughter; the eyes are as open as his heart. Poor Raistlin.*

Par-Salian turned his gaze back to the young man whose red robes hung from thin, stooped shoulders. Obviously weak, Raistlin was the one who could never take what he wanted, so he had learned, long ago, that magic could compensate for his deficiencies. Par-Salian looked into his eyes. No, they were not mirrors as the master had said – not for those with the power to see deeply. There was good inside the young man – an inner core of strength that would enable his fragile body to endure much. But now his soul was a cold, shapeless mass, dark with pride, greed, and selfishness. Therefore, as a shapeless mass of metal is plunged into a white-hot fire and emerges shining steel, so Par-Salian intended to forge this conjurer.

'Your brother cannot stay,' the Mage admonished softly.

'I am aware of that, Great One,' Raistlin replied, with a hint of impatience.

'He will be well cared for in your absence,' Par-Salian continued. 'And of course, he will be allowed to carry home your valuables should the Test prove beyond your skill.'

'Carry home . . . valuables . . . ' Caramon's face became grim as he considered this statement. Then it darkened as he understood the full meaning of the Mage's words. 'You mean –'

Raistlin's voice cut in, sharp, edged. 'He means, dear brother, that you will take home my possessions in the event of my death.'

Par-Salian shrugged.

'Failure, invariably, proves fatal.'

'Yes, you're right. I forgot that death could be a result of this . . . ritual.' Caramon's face crumped into wrinkles of fear. He laid his hand on his brother's arm. 'I think you should forget this, Raist. Let's go home.'

Raistlin twitched at his brother's touch, his thin body shuddering. 'Do I counsel you to refuse battle?' he flared. Then, controlling his anger, he continued more calmly. 'This is my battle, Caramon. Do not worry. I will not fail.'

Caramon pleaded. 'Please, Raist . . . I'm supposed to take care of you –'

'Leave me!' Raistlin's control cracked, splintered, wounding his brother.

Caramon fell backward. 'All right,' he mumbled. 'I'll . . . I'll meet you . . . outside.' He flashed the Mage a threatening glance. Then he turned and walked out of the chamber, his huge battlesword clanking against his thigh.

A door thudded, then there was silence.

'I apologize for my brother,' Raistlin said, his lips barely moving.

'Do you?' Par-Salian asked. 'Why?'

The young man scowled. 'Because he always . . . Oh, can't we just get on with this?' His hands clenched beneath the sleeves of his robe.

'Of course,' the Mage replied, leaning back in his chair. Raistlin stood straight, eyes open and unblinking. Then he drew in a sharp breath.

The Mage made a gesture. There was a sound, a shattering crack. Quickly, the conjurer vanished.

A voice spoke from the nether regions. 'Why must we test this one so severely?'

Par-Salian's twisted hands clasped and unclasped. 'Who questions the gods?' He frowned. 'They demanded a sword. I found one, but his metal is white hot. He must be beaten . . . tempered . . . made useful.'

'And if he breaks?'

'Then we will bury the pieces,' murmured the Mage.

Raistlin dragged himself away from the dead body of the dark elf. Wounded and exhausted, he crawled into a shadowy corridor and slumped against a wall. Pain twisted him. He clutched his stomach and retched. When the convulsion subsided, he lay back on the stone floor and waited for death.

Why are they doing this to me? he wondered through a dreamy haze of pain. Only a young conjurer, he had been subjected to trials devised by the most renowned Mages – living and dead. The fact that he must pass these Tests was no longer his main thought; survival, however, was. Each trial had wounded him, and his health had always been precarious. If he survived this ordeal – and he doubted he would – he could imagine his body to be like a shattered crystal, held together by the force of his own will.

But then, of course, there was Caramon, who would care for him – as always.

Ha! The thought penetrated the haze, even made Raistlin laugh harshly. No, death was preferable to a life of dependence on his brother. Raistlin lay back on the stone floor, wondering how much longer they would let him suffer . . .

. . . And a huge figure materialized out of the shadowy darkness of the corridor.

This is it, Raistlin thought, *my final test. The one I won't survive.*

He decided simply not to fight, even though he had one spell left. Maybe death would be quick and merciful.

He lay on his back, staring at the dark shadow as it drew closer and closer. It came to stand next to him. He could sense its living presence, hear its breathing. It bent over him. Involuntarily, he closed his eyes.

'Raist?'

He felt cold fingers touch his burning flesh.

'Raist!' the voice sobbed. 'In the name of the gods, what have they done to you?'

'Caramon,' Raistlin spoke, but he couldn't hear his own voice. His throat was raw from coughing.

'I'm taking you out of here,' his brother announced firmly.

Raistlin felt strong arms slip under his body. He smelled the familiar smell of sweat and leather, heard the familiar sound of armour creak and broadsword clank.

'No!' Raistlin pushed against his brother's massive chest with a frail, fragile hand. 'Leave me, Caramon! My tests are not complete! Leave me!' His voice was an inaudible croak, then he gagged violently.

Caramon lifted him easily, cradled him in his arms. 'Nothing is worth this. Rest easy, Raist.' The big man choked. As they walked under a flickering torch, Caramon could see tears on his brother's cheeks. He made one last effort.

'They won't allow us to go, Caramon!' He raised his head, gasping for breath. 'You're only putting yourself in danger!'

'Let them come,' Caramon said grimly, walking with firm steps down the dimly lit corridor.

Raistlin sank back, helpless, his head resting on Caramon's shoulder. He felt comforted by his brother's strength, though he cursed him inwardly.

You fool! Raistlin closed his eyes wearily. *You great, stubborn fool! Now we'll both die. And, of course, you will die protecting me. Even in death I'll be indebted to you!*

'Ah . . .'

Raistlin heard and felt the sharp intake of breath into his brother's body. Caramon's walk had slowed. Raistlin raised his head and peered ahead.

'A wraith,' he breathed.

'Mmmmm . . . ' Caramon rumbled deeply in his chest – his battle-cry.

'My magic can destroy it,' Raistlin protested as Caramon laid him gently on the stone floor. *Burning Hands*, Raistlin thought grimly. A weak spell against a wraith, but he had to try. 'Move, Caramon! I have just enough strength left.'

Caramon did not answer. He turned around and walked toward the wraith, blocking Raistlin's view.

Clinging to the wall, the conjurer clawed his way to a standing position and raised his hand. Just as he was about to expend his strength in one last shout, hoping to warn off his brother, he stopped and stared in disbelief. Caramon raised his hand. Where before he had held a sword, now he held a rod of amber. In the other hand, his shield hand, he held a bit of fur. He rubbed the two together, spoke some magic words – and a lightening bolt flashed, striking the wraith in the chest. It shrieked, but kept coming, intent on draining Caramon's life energy. Caramon kept his hands raised. He spoke again. Another bolt sizzled, catching the wraith in its head. And suddenly there was nothing.

'Now we'll get out of here,' Caramon said with satisfaction. The rod and the fur were gone. He turned around. 'The door is just ahead – '

'How did you do that?' Raistlin asked, propping himself up against the wall.

Caramon halted, alarmed by his brother's wild, frenzied stare.

'Do what!' The fighter blinked.

'The magic!' Raistlin shrieked in fury. 'The magic!'

'Oh, that,' Caramon shrugged. 'I've always been able to. Most of the time I don't need it, what with my sword and all, but you're hurt real bad and I've got to get you out of here. I didn't want to take time fighting that character. Don't bother about it, Raist. It can still be your little speciality. Like I said before, most of the time I don't need it.'

This is impossible, Raistlin's mind told him. *He couldn't have acquired in moments what it took me years of study to attain. This doesn't make sense. Fight the sickness and the weakness and the pain! Think!* But it wasn't the physical pain that clouded Raistlin's mind. It was the old inner pain clawing at him, tearing at him with poisoned talons. Caramon, strong and cheerful, good and kind, open and honest. Everyone's friend.

Not like Raistlin – the runt, the Sly One.

All I ever had was my magic, Raistlin's mind shrieked. *And now he has that too!*

Propping himself against the wall for support, Raistlin raised both his hands, put his thumbs together, and pointed them at Caramon. He began murmuring magic words, but different from those that Caramon had spoken.

'Raist?' Caramon backed up. 'What are you doing? C'mon! Let me help you. I'll take care of you – just like always . . . Raist! I'm your brother!'

Raistlin's parched lips cracked in a grin. Hatred and jealousy – long kept bubbling and molten beneath a layer of cold, solid rock – burst forth. Magic coursed through his body and flamed out of his hands. He watched the fire flare, billow, and engulf Caramon. When the fighter became a living torch, Raistlin suddenly knew from his training that what he was seeing simply could not be. The instant that he realized something was wrong with this occurrence, the burning image of his brother vanished. A moment later, Raistlin lost consciousness and slumped to the ground.

'Awaken, Raistlin, your trials are complete.'

Raistlin opened his eyes. The darkness was gone; sunshine streamed through a window. He lay in a bed. Looking down at him was the withered face of Par-Salian.

'Why?' Raistlin rasped, clutching at the Mage in fury. 'Why did you do that to me?'

Par-Salian laid his hand on the frail young man's shoulder. 'The gods asked for a sword, Raistlin, and now I can give them one – you. Evil is coming upon the land. The fate of all this world called Krynn swings in the balance. Through the aid of your hand and others, the balance will be restored.'

Raistlin stared, then laughed, briefly and bitterly. 'Save Krynn? How? You have shattered my body. I can't even see properly!' He stared in terror . . .

. . . For, as Raistlin watched, he could see the Mage's face dying. When he turned his gaze to the window, the stones he looked at crumbled before his eyes. Wherever he looked, everything was falling into ruin and decay. Then, the moment passed, and his vision cleared.

Par-Salian handed him a mirror. Raistlin saw that his own face was sunken and hollow. His skin was a golden colour now, with a faint metallic cast; this would be a symbol of the agony he had endured. But it was his eyes that caused him to recoil in horror, for the black pupils were no longer round – they were the shape of hourglasses!

'You see through hourglass eyes now, Raistlin. And so you see time, as it touches all things. You see death, whenever you look on life. Thus you will always be aware of the brief timespan, we spend in the world.' Par-Salian shook his head. 'There will be no joy in your life, Raistlin, I fear – indeed, little joy for anyone living on Krynn.'

Raistlin laid the mirror face down. 'My brother?' he asked, his voice barely a whisper.

'It was an illusion that I created – my personal challenge for you to look deeper into your own heart and examine the ways in which you deal with those closest to you,' Par-Salian said gently. 'As for your brother, he is here, safe . . . quite safe. Here he comes now.'

As Caramon entered the room, Raistlin sat up, shoving Par-Salian aside. The warrior appeared relieved to see that his twin had enough energy to greet him, but Caramon's eyes reflected a certain sadness that comes from learning an unpleasant truth.

'I didn't think you would recognize the illusion for what it was,' Par-Salian said. 'But you did; after all, what magic-user can work spells, carrying a sword and wearing armour?'

'Then I did not fail?' Raistlin murmured hoarsely.

'No.' Par-Salian smiled. The final of the Test was the defeat of the dark elf – truly superb for one of your experience.'

Raistlin looked at his brother's haunted face, his averted eyes. 'He watched me kill him, didn't he?' Raistlin whispered.

'Yes,' Par-Salian looked from one to the other. 'I am sorry I had to do this to you, Raistlin. You have much to learn, mage – mercy, compassion, forebearance. It is my hope that the trials you face ahead of you will teach you what you lack now. If not, you will succumb in the end to the fate your master foresaw. But, as of now, you and your brother truly know each other. The barriers between you have been battered down, though I am afraid each of you has suffered wounds in the encounter. I hope the scars make you stronger.'

Par-Salian rose to leave. 'Use you powers well, mage. The time is close at hand when your strength must save the world.'

Raistlin bowed his head and sat in silence until Par-Salian had left the room. Then he stood up, staggered, and nearly fell.

Caramon jumped forward to help him, but Raistlin, clinging to the wooden staff, caught himself. Fighting the pain and dizziness that assailed him. Raistlin's golden-eyed gaze met that of his twin. Caramon hesitated . . . and stopped.

Raistlin sighed. Then, learning on the Staff of Magius, the young mage pulled himself upright and walked, slowly and with faltering steps, out the door.

Head bowed, his twin followed.

Spinning the Green

Margaret Elphinstone

Once upon a time there lived a rich merchant. He had three daughters called Elsie, Lacie and Tilly, and they lived on the profits of a treacle mine. Elsie and Lacie were not clearly differentiated in the minds of anybody, they were just elder sisters, and from that you can draw your own conclusions. Tilly was as kind as she was good, and as good as she was beautiful, and as beautiful as she was kind. And if that doesn't tell you what you want to know, swallow your subversive curiousity and read on.

Now the merchant had been worried for some time, for shares in treacle had been falling rapidly, as a result of a cruel government campaign which forced him to add Treacle Rots Your Teeth in letters no less that one millimetre high on every billboard advertising treacle. Also, the matter of spoil heaps had recently become a sticky issue in the environmentalist press. So the merchant saddled his horse one day, and called his daughters to kiss him goodbye and wish him well, for he was setting out to an international convention to establish the future secure foundations of the treacle industry.

Before he set spurs to his horse, however, he turned to his daughters and said, 'Is there any little gift you would like me to bring you when I come home again?'

'Diamonds,' said Elsie, her eyes gleaming. 'Diamonds, gold, pineapples, peaches, oranges and sherry, and two tickets to a cricket match.'

'Coffee,' said Lacie, smiling sweetly. 'Coffee, chocolate, tobacco, soya, nuts, beef and a tract of primeval forest.'

'And Tilly my dear,' said the merchant fondly. 'What about you?'

And Tilly, for reasons of her own which will become apparent later, replied, 'A red rose, Papa, if you please.'

The convention was moderately successful. The merchant was not entirely happy. He had an obscure feeling that he was being duped by his partners from across the Western Sea, and he wasn't keen on the new policy of exporting guns hidden at the bottom of the treacle barrels. So he rode home slowly with a slack rein, passing unseeing through the perilous tracks of the Wild Forest, while little graphs flashed across the grey screens of his mind, and square green digits bleeped continuously through his thoughts.

The horse had other ideas. (It is important to remember that, because the world does not change by chance.)

When the merchant looked up again, he found himself in a part of the forest he had never seen before, a wild perilous growing place, where the trees crowded so thickly that the dead trunks were held up by their living neighbours. Strange matted creepers hung from branches far above, while curious rustlings and calls echoed through the undergrowth. The merchant found it wild, and shuddered. He was utterly lost.

'We are utterly lost,' he said to his horse, who naturally did not contradict him.

At that moment an arrow embedded itself in the merchant's saddle-bow.

Yes, an arrow.

The merchant registered a faint thud, and saw it quivering, inches from his hand. His eyes widened, and slowly he raised his arms above his head, hoping that was the correct thing to do under these unusual circumstances. The arrow was a yard long and had a green feather. The horse took a step forward and began to crop the long sweet grass.

'How do you do?' called the merchant quaveringly, when the silence grew too intense.

As soon as he spoke two figures appeared, swinging lightly

from low branches that overhung the path. They stood, arrows notched, one behind him and one before, so that there was no way left to turn. They were both clad from head to foot in garb of Lincoln green.

'I have no money,' gasped the merchant, 'and even if I had it would be against my principles to acquiesce in so subversive an activity as the redistribution of wealth. I have always paid my taxes, and if you don't believe me I will vouchsafe to you my national insurance number, so that you can dial the police computer and check that I am a responsible citizen, and find out everything you wish to know about me and a great deal more which you would be a fool to believe anyway. Please do not threaten me with violence. I have a place in a fallout shelter which cost me a great deal, and it would be most unfortunate if it were wasted. Will you let me go now if I offer to send you a consignment of treacle?'

They ignored this speech completely. The one in front of him lowered her bow and came near enough for the horse to nuzzle her face. 'We have come to invite you to dinner,' she said.

They blindfolded him and led him to their camp by many secret ways. The dinner was excellent, though the merchant could have eaten something a little more substantial than fresh fruits and herbs of the forest. He reckoned there must be at least two score of the women in green. There was no trace of any man among them, and yet they totally ignored him. Their children joined in the feast without hindrance, running freely round the clearing, returning to help themselve from high piled dishes, disappearing under the trees so that shrill laughter rang from the shadows. Above the merchant's head the green canopy of branches appeared to dance and flicker in the firelight. Between the leaves he saw the still cold points of stars looking indifferently down upon him. His horse was gone.

Only the two women who had captured him took notice of him. They treated him well, bringing him food and drink, and even condescending to talk to him a little. They asked nothing of him, and threatened him not at all, but that in itself made him uneasy. Finally he raised the subject that troubled him. 'Do you wish me to pay the bill?'

'There is no bill.'

A few minutes later he tried again, under the guise of light conversation. 'Am I right in thinking that your organization is dedicated to the recirculation of capital?'

'There is no organization.'

Apparently they insisted upon direct speech. 'Presumably you want my money?'

'We want no money.'

Incredulous, he tried to understand. 'Then what do you want?'

'Nothing you cannot give.'

Was that a threat? Trembling, he said, 'Then don't torture me. If you will let me go free, I will give whatever you ask.'

'You have no need to fear. What we want from you, no woman ever took from man by force.'

After that they left him, and fearful thoughts troubled him.

He began to grow strangely sleepy. The voices of the women and the interlacing branches above him seemed to weave together into bizarre patterns. The children were silent, or departed, and the women were sitting in a wide circle. Their voices rose and fell, and their hands were busy. Across the firelight he saw that they were spinning, spinning green threads, green threads twining together, spindles growing heavy with green. He watched neat fingers twisting the thread, and then weaving it, a green web woven, the circle of spinners become a circle of weavers. They spun the thread and wove the web, and the merchant's eyes grew sleepier, his head heavier, and he could watch the weaving of the web no longer. Only the voices drifted on into his dreams, weaving words to and fro across the circle:

> 'Who else is there now
> Can spin the green
> To cover the earth anew?'

Languorous sleep engulfed him, there was a scent like wild thyme in the air. He dreamed he was on a bank soft with oxslips, strewn with violets, and over his head musk roses shone palely in the moonlight, and around their stems grew a matted canopy of eglantine. He slept.

He woke in the cold light of dawn, and the shreds of wild sensuous dreams fled before his rising consciousness. Regretfully he sat up and rubbed his eyes. He was sitting in the place where the archers had ambushed him, and beside him lay his pack, untouched, with his cloak and saddle and bridle. No horse. Stiffly he got to his feet, aware now of a slight ache in his loins, but of no other hurt at all. In fact he felt curiously light, more relaxed in his body than usual. Yet his plight could hardly be worse. He was lost and far from home and his horse was gone.

He sighed and picked up his saddlebags. They were depressingly heavy: Elsie and Lacie's presents were not light. That made him think affectionately of his youngest daughter, and at the same moment a mass of tangled briars caught his eye, studded all over with delicate wild roses. Red roses. The merchant reached up painfully under the weight of his pack, pulled down a branch, and, ignoring the thorns that tore at his fingers, he picked a stem heavy with bright flowers.

They were enraged shouts and footsteps behind him. He turned to see the two women, their bows once more bent against him.

'I beg your pardon,' he stammered, and the roses trembled on the stem clutched in his hand.

'How dare you?' Their wrath was terrifying. 'How dare you, after we have treated you well and let you leave unharmed. How dare you pick the roses? Must you destroy every living thing that you find growing freely? How dare you do such a thing here?'

'I beg your pardon,' he said again. 'I meant no harm. The roses were for my daughter, Tilly. She asked me to bring her back a rose. Really, it wasn't my idea at all.'

'We are very angry,' said the other. 'You have no right to pick the roses.'

'Please do not kill me.' The merchant fell to his knees, his head bowed, and so failed to see the glance that passed between the women. 'It was my daughter's wish. I never meant to anger you. My other daughters have all that they asked for here in my pack. Tilly asked only for a rose. What can I do to save my life?'

'There is only one thing you can do now.' Her voice was scornful. 'You can send your daughter here in your place. If you can persuade her to do that, and bring her back within thirteen cycles of the moon, then we will not pursue you, but will let you live as you will in your own place for ever. But if she does not come, you can be very sure that you will be sent for, and there will be no further escape. So be warned!'

'Very well,' gabbled the merchant. 'I promise you I can persuade her. She will come if I explain it to her. I will see to it that she comes.'

The women said no more, and when the merchant dared to glance up they were gone. Trembling, he shouldered his pack once more, and set out to find his way home.

Tilly was the first to see her father returning. She was weeding the front garden, while her sisters were indoors reading romances and eating liquorice allsorts. Tilly dropped her fork and called to them. 'It's Papa home, and he's lost his horse.'

'Lost his horse? How dreadful! I wonder if he has our presents then?' Elsie and Lacie hurried out to see.

Soon the three sisters surrounded the weary merchant, begging him to tell them what had happened, how had he lost his horse, what misadventures had befallen him.

The merchant mentally reviewed his story. It did not sound particularly heroic, especially as there was still a slight numbness in his balls which suggested that something terribly embarrassing had happened to him. He cleared his throat, thinking fast, and told his story.

'Alas, alas, dear daughters,' he began. 'I was wending my weary way home, thinking only of you, my loved ones, when by mischance I lost myself in the Wild Forest. Exhausted and afraid though I was, I pressed ever onward, knowing that therein lay my only hope of returning to comfort my beloved children. Then suddenly . . . ' Here he paused and looked around wildly for inspiration. 'Suddenly I heard an unearthly roaring behind me. The ground shook, the birds took to the air in clamorous terror, the very flowers by the wayside wilted and dropped their heads. There sprang out in front of me a hideous Beast, an image more vile than anything I had beheld in wildest nightmare, a loathsome brute of indescribable ugliness. With a fearful roar he seized me . . . ' He saw his daughters looking curiously at his unscarred form clad with customary neatness. 'However, his grip was astonishingly gentle. He took me to his palace in the heart of the wood, and vanished from my sight.'

'How very odd,' said Tilly thoughtfully.

'How simply dreadful, Papa,' cried Elsie and Lacie. 'How noble and brave you are. No one else would dare to go where you have gone. What happened then?'

The merchant began to perceive a flaw in this re-telling of his tale. He gave Tilly an appraising glance and changed his tone a little. 'The palace in the forest was strange and beautiful, a place of enchantment. Invisible hands fed me with ambrosial delicacies, invisible guides led me to a luxurious bedroom. I had but to wish for any mortal thing and it was brought to me: exotic fruits and wines, fresh linen clothes, a colour television with six channels, and mysteriously scented chemicals to put in the sunken bath. Even the toilet seat was lined with white fur.'

'Good gracious!'

'The next morning I found myself alone. My breakfast was neatly laid, so that I only had to plug in the coffee pot and put the sliced bread in the toaster. I ate my fill, and left a note of thanks by the emerald-studded telephone. I found my way out through delightful gardens, between beds filled with the brightest flowers I ever beheld. At the gate I chanced upon a bush covered with red roses. At once I remembered you, dear Tilly. I reached and picked a spray of roses.' The merchant paused dramatically.

'What happened to your horse?' asked Tilly.

Her sisters silenced her at once. 'How can you be so unfeeling? See what our poor father has suffered, and you ask about a horse! Go on, dear Papa, go on.' Their eyes were hopefully fixed upon his pack.

'Immediately I heard again that terrible roaring. Again the ground shook, and the Beast appeared before me, more hideous than ever in the clear light of day. I confess I quailed before him. He towered over me, threatening me with huge talons and growling furiously. "I will kill you at once," he shrieked. "For I have treated you well and in return you have dared to pick my roses. For this you must die! I will tear you limb from limb forthwith!'

' "Oh please don't," I said as bravely as I could. "I have three daughters waiting for me at home, and if you eat me, whatever is to become of them? They will starve in the gutter, or somewhere similar, and there will be no one to succour them in their distress!" '

'And did he listen?'

The merchant brushed away a tear. 'Alas, dear Tilly, how am I to tell you this? He said he would let me go on one condition: that I bring you back within thirteen cycles of the moon, in my place.' He glanced at Tilly again. 'He said you could live in luxury in his palace, waited on hand and foot, and that he would provide you with anything you desired. But go there you must, and stay there at his pleasure.'

'So I should think,' said Elsie. 'After all, it was her that wanted the rose.'

'It doesn't sound a bad life to me,' said Lacie. 'And you could always try kissing him. He might turn into a handsome prince.'

'I'd rather he turned into a frog,' said Tilly. 'Papa, did he kill the horse.'

'My brave girl,' said the merchant, embracing her fondly. 'I knew you would never fail me. Let us be happy together while we still may. What have you prepared for dinner?'

A year later.

Tilly waited patiently by the rose bush. Her father had bidden her a fond but hasty farewell, and now she was sitting quietly on the ground, a little puzzled that there was no trace of any garden or palace, but not particularly afraid. Birds called through the wood, and a couple of green dragonflies fluttered in the sunshine. Tall trees towered around her, and narrow paths disappeared into tangled undergrowth. A warm inhabited place, but not tamed. She did not feel far from her own kind, but there was no trace of man. Then who?'

She thought about the Beast, and frowned. This strange offer of a life of luxury, tainted by the threat of violence. A Beast that wanted her, who would provide her with her heart's desire, yet force her to his will. Whose anger was turned against her, because she had wanted a gift innocently gained. Who said that even the flowers of the forest belonged to him, and who could have her delivered into his power by mere command. Such a creature must be incredible, had she not learned its nature from her own father. Tilly shrugged, and went on waiting.

She couldn't remember falling asleep, but when she opened her eyes, women in green stood around her, their bows slung across their backs. She stared, and silently they stared back.

'I'm Tilly,' she said at last. 'I am my father's ransom.'

They nodded, as if they had expected her, and signed to her to follow them.

They took her to the clearing in the forest, and brought her food and water, and gave her a bed of fern to lie on, sheltered under green branches. They were silent, but not invisible. Tilly supposed the enchantment was done differently for her, and waited for the Beast to come. But he did not come, not that day, or the next, or the next.

At night she had dreams.

She would fall asleep looking at the patterns woven by leaves over her head, and her dreams were of green threads spinning, and a green web woven around her by many hands; a circle of spinners invisible under the stars, a circle of weavers with the green web stretched vibrant between their hands. Voices twined through her dreams, the singing of the spinners. And out of the weaving of words she caught a few lines circling, which wove their way through to her waking thoughts, so that she remembered them in the morning:

> 'Who else is there now
> Can spin the green
> To cover the earth anew?'

She woke thinking of a place her father owned where the wind blew across scarred soil until red rock showed, where once a forest stood. She thought of the red rose she had asked for, which had brought her to this place. When the women came with her breakfast she was waiting for them.

'Where is the Beast?' she asked.

For the first time one of the women spoke to her.

'The Beast has gone home,' she said quietly, and left.

The next day Tilly tried again. 'Where is the Beast?' she asked.

This time another woman answered.

'We are the Beast,' she said, and went away.

That was no help, but Tilly was ready to try again. 'Where is the Beast?' she asked on the third day.

'The Beast is in your head,' said the third woman, and departed.

Tilly sat with her hands pressed to her head and thought. Why had her father not told her the truth? To save himself embarrassment? If that were more important to him than the fate of his daughter then things she had taken for granted all her life must be considered again. Clear anger began to grow in her, welling up like cold water out of the earth, sweeping away the dust of lies and obligations which had so long engulfed her. She leapt to her feet and strode out into the deserted clearing, and called with all her strength into the silent hidden forest.

'There is no Beast,' she shouted, and the leaves stirred above her in the sun. 'THERE IS NO BEAST.'

The women came.

They ran from the dimness under the trees and surrounded her, spoke to her with friendly voices, looked at her with understanding eyes. If there ever were enchantment, she had broken it. And if anything were real, it was as she saw it, for the power of any man's nightmare is gone when there is no one left to believe in it.

As the women led her to their camp, she heard in the distance the thud of unshod hooves, and the neighing of wild horses.

The seasons passed, and Tilly learned what it was she needed from the forest, and she learned also what the forest needed from her. She found out who she was, but that cannot be told outside the wood, not yet. Her clothes were now woven of green cloth, for she too became a Spinner. And in the spinning she came to know her companions, as herself.

The roses were flowering again on the briar bushes, and Tilly thought again of her father. She asked the women how she might get news of him, and they directed her to a well of seeing.

The first thing she saw was her sisters. They had strayed into the fringes of the forest, and stumbling on the edges of another world had fortuitously ended up in the arms of two young men, Lysander and Demetrius. Rather than come face to face with the unknown they had married them forthwith, almost before the two couples had had time to tell one another apart. She saw her father, relieved, at the double wedding. If her sisters had encountered subversive passions in the Wild Forest, they were neatly tied up now, and any sense of wistfulness could be projected on to Lysander, or Demetrius, or anywhere else where the grass looked greener.

As for her father, he went home alone, and fell prey to various undiagnosed complaints. His doctor wrote him off in his file as depressed, possible neurotic, and prescribed tranquillizers. The merchant began to drink too much, and was soon in a bad way, as Tilly saw in the well of seeing.

So she went to visit him. The night before she left the women warned her, 'Don't stay past one cycle of the moon, or you too will change, and maybe never come back at all.'

Tilly heard their warning, but when she got home she found life more absorbing than she had expected. Her father cheered up wonderfully, and she helped him sort out his affairs and plan an early retirement. This included booking a round-the-world cruise avoiding winter everywhere, and building a new swimming pool in the garden. Her sisters also required her sympathy on the problems of relating to men and married life. She knew it was her duty to listen to them, as her freedom was so obviously painful to them. All in all, nearly two months had gone by when there came a night of storm which blew the late summer leaves from the trees. The sound of the wind penetrated Tilly's sleep. She dreamed of things dying and forgotten, and in the centre of nightmare she saw a green web broken, and a world where there were no more trees.

First thing next morning she went to the well and said a spell of seeing. She saw no visions and heard no pleas. But a voice came from the depths, cool and clear, asking for nothing:

'Sister, the choice is yours.'

Within the hour she had said farewell to her father and sisters. She told her father she would come again when he really needed her. She told her sisters that if ever they wished they were free to come and find her. Then she left them, and was soon lost to sight, a woman in green among green trees.

The Mist on the Moor

Diana L. Paxson

Mist swirled across the path like a tattered shroud, choking the breath as it blinded the eye. Shanna swore and reined in, too sharply – Calur slipped on wet rock and nearly fell, then stood shuddering. The falcon, Chai, mantled with a wild fluttering of wings, and settled back to the saddlebrow, scolding harshly.

'Oh be still!' Shanna told her. 'We have to get through this wasteland before sundown.' She did not allow herself to think what would happen if they did not. She did not allow herself to articulate the fact that they were lost already, going on only because she had always kept going, whether or not she knew her way.

Chai responded with another protest, then her mottled russet feathers folded back into sleekness, and powerful talons fastened once more on the scarred leather of the saddle. Shanna could still hear a muffled grumbling from deep in the bird's throat, and was momentarily glad that the falcon no longer had the power to assume her human form.

The curse of one emperor had doomed Chai's kin, and Shanna feared that the treachery of another had caused her own brother to disappear. After the escort with which she had started her journey had been killed, Shanna had thought that there would be some comfort in sharing her quest with Chai, but at this moment the burden of her own fate was almost more than she could bear. Imprisoned in bird form, Chai was only a mute reminder of an additional responsibility. *Don't think*, Shanna told herself. *Just keep on* . . .

She stood up in the stirrups, trying to peer ahead, but mist had swallowed up the world. Settling back into the saddle, she took up her reins and squeezed the mare's sides with her long legs to get her moving again. Calur whickered unhappily, took one lurching step forward, and then halted.

'Turds!' Shanna was already swinging out of the saddle as she swore. Swiftly she ran callused fingers down the mare's leg, felt her flinch as she probed the pastern, and straightened with another obscenity. Her mind strained against the fear of being trapped here as her eyes had strained to see through the mist that surrounded her.

They had to keep going, she told herself as she gave a gentle tug to the rein. The moor could not extend forever. Still limping, but not so badly without a rider, the mare followed her. Shanna bit her lip, refusing to recognize the panic that surged within. She was a princess of Sharteyn, and she had sworn to complete this journey. That was the only thing she could allow herself to remember now.

'Holy Yraine,' she murmured. 'Let me see my way!'

She hitched her swordbelt higher and rubbed at the aching muscles in her lower back, and kept walking. But still the mist curled and eddied around her. The silver light was unchanging – she could not tell if any time had passed, if there was any time, here. One of her boots had burst a seam, letting in moisture with every puddle she stepped in. Shanna's foot slid in clammy leather, and she stumbled, dropped the rein to avoid hurting the mare's mouth, and sprawled in the mud.

'Misbegotten muck!' For a moment she lay where she had fallen, furious and exhausted. Then she felt the mud dragging her down and, panicking, pushed herself upright. Calur took a limping step toward her, lowered her head and butted Shanna anxiously.

'It's your fault, you bay bitch!' Shanna struck out at her. The mare whickered unhappily and shied back, and Shanna felt despair drown her fury and sighed, looking around her. At ground level, the fog veiled a wilderness of heather whose belled blooms were lightly pearled by the air's moisture, but she could not appreciate their beauty. She shivered, and gathered her strength to get up again. It was cold for late summer; at least walking would keep her warm.

Still half-crouched, she paused, staring down, then straightened to her full lean height. Chai called questioningly.

'Did you see it too?' she asked the falcon. 'If only you could still talk!' The falcon shifted position on the saddlebow, and Shanna stroked her bronze feathers gently, still looking down.

She had not imagined it – water was seeping into a human footprint in the mud before her. She had seen no one, but this thick mist could hide anything, and the footprint was fresh . . . Her vision blurred and she twitched a strand of black hair out of her eyes, but it didn't help much. Hope fluttered like a trapped bird in her heart as she tried to steady her voice.

'Come on, girl, whoever made this print can't have gotten very far. We'll find him and he'll set us on the right path.'

She tugged at the reins and stumbled down the track, following the footprints. And in a few moments she knew that she had finally done something right, for she smelled the smoke of a wood fire.

But it was hard to say where the mist ended and the smoke began. A shape loomed before her, she started to hurry and stubbed her toes on an outcropping of stone. In the end, it was not her own senses, but Calur's hopeful whicker that told her when they finally came to the house she was looking for.

The place would have been easy to miss – weathered boards and a roof of cut turf overgrown with grass made it look like part of the moor. But the ground was flatter around it, and the wiry growth had been somewhat discouraged by the passage of human feet. A soft, background clucking indicated the presence of fowl.

Shanna threw back the hood of her red cloak and took a deep breath, then she tugged on Calur's rein and, wincing as her weight came down on her bruised toes, marched around the wall to find the front door. She could hear no sound from inside, and there was no response to her knocking. But she did smell something cooking behind that sagging door, and abruptly her stomach would let her delay no longer. She dropped Calur's rein, held out her arm so that Chai could run up it to perch on her shoulder, and pushed the door open.

An old woman was bent, stirring, over a pot that stood on three legs above the peat fire. On the other side of the cottage, as far away as he could get and still remain in the same room, a man was sitting in a rough chair. His back was to the door and all Shanna could see of him was one outstretched leg and the top of a balding head, but his foot was about the size of the prints she had seen. She wondered what these two old people were doing out here alone.

She coughed, and took two steps into the room.

At almost the same moment, the door blew shut behind her, and the old man and woman turned and looked at her with bright stars like the avid eyes of birds. These eyes held not the proud gaze of Chai's people, but something more akin to the faintly malicious intelligence of a raven or a swan. Chai shifted restlessly on her shoulder, and she wondered what the falcon thought of their hosts. Such a look in human faces was oddly disturbing, but Shanna had faced worse. She forced a smile.

'My horse went lame, and I need to a place to rest her. May we shelter with you for a little while?'

For a moment the old woman said nothing. Then she cocked her head toward the man.

'Yod, you fool! I told you something like this would happen if you went out today!' She wiped her hands on the rusty black folds of her gown.

'You told me to go, you old besom – that's what you told me! It's your stinking herbs I went out to gather, wasn't it? Sitting right there in that basket that someone will trip over if you don't put it away!' The chair scraped as he turned it to face the hearth. His white beard flowed down his chest like an animal's pelt.

'Those herbs grow beside the stream, not on the high moor, and you know it well, old man.' The woman waggled her finger at him. Her hair was still dark beneath its threading of grey, while the man's was pure silver, but as she turned, the firelight flared full on her face, and Shanna saw that it was seamed and crinkled like last autumn's leaves.

'What were you doing up there, leaving footmarks for anyone who came along to follow? Up to no good, I'll be bound!' she went on.

Shanna stared. How did the old women know that she had followed the man down from the moor? After that first look, the old creature hardly seemed to be aware that anyone else was in the room.

'I know who you've been meeting up there, you old lecher – ' The woman gave the pot a vigorous stir. 'Enjoy it while you can, for winter's coming, and she'll be gone with the rest of the flock!'

Shanna coughed. 'Pardon me, Grandmother, but the day is passing – if I can't stay here, I must be on my way. May I claim your hospitality?'

'Claim?' The old woman looked at her finally, her eyes glittering like dark coals. 'You cannot claim anything, child, but you may ask . . . '

'I ask you then.' Painfully Shanna bent in a court bow. 'Lady, of your mercy, I beg shelter!'

The old woman grinned, and her face folded into a thousand creases, like a map of barren watercourses in a dry land. 'So – manners are not entirely dead among the young! I am glad to see it. Stable your mare in the shed behind the cottage,' she added abruptly. 'And you, my daughter, may stay here with me.'

Shanna turned her head and met Chai's fixed golden stare. There was some meaning in that look, but the curse upon the falcon's people prevented her from voicing it. However Chai moved onto the old woman's arm readily enough, so Shanna had to conclude that whatever the falcon had sensed about their hostess was nothing dangerous.

When Shanna returned from settling Calur, Chai was perched upon the mantel of the hearth, preening her bronze feathers. Steaming bowls had been set upon the rough table, and the old man was already seated, spooning up stew noisily. It sounded as though he was straining it through his beard, but the white mat remained miraculously unstained.

The woman pointed, and Shanna took a place beside him. The scent of the stew filled the air, redolent of onions, and chicken, and some kind of spice she could not identify. She told herself that she should taste just a little at first; there was too much that was strange here for her to trust what came out of the old woman's mouth or her cauldron without testing it, but her stomach reminded her how long it had been since she had eaten, and once she had taken the first bite, Shanna found herself gobbling as fast as the old man.

Shanna stared at the bottom of the bowl, and realized that she had been looking at it, seeing nothing, for some time. Or perhaps her eyes had been closed – she blinked rapidly, trying to clear her head. She had eaten one bowlful, or perhaps it was more, she could not quite remember, and the room was very warm. She was not used to feeding so well, and digestion was claiming all her energy. In that muzzy warmth, even the aching of bruised feet and muscles made sore by unaccustomed walking faded away.

Her head drooped and she brought herself upright with a start. Why was she so sleepy? Chai was still perched on the mantel, eyes hooded as if she were dozing already. Shanna wondered what the old woman had fed *her*. The old man had disappeared, but she did not think he had gone far, for his staff was still leaning against the wall beside the door. As she looked around, the old grandmother came through a door she had not noticed before, her arms piled her with blankets.

'Here, child, you may make up your bed before the fire. We old folks need our rest, so you must forgive me for not keeping you company. We will talk when morning comes.'

Shanna stared at her, suspecting irony – at the moment, the old lady seemed to be far more alert than she was. But the woman was already spreading the blankets in front of the hearth.

The natural grey wool looked liked carded clouds. Soft clouds – so soft – Shanna knelt to feel their texture, and then somehow she was lying down, and the old woman was pulling another over her.

'Thank you,' she murmured. 'Thank you – what shall I call you?' Fatigue thickened her tongue.

'You may call me Ama – ' The old woman's voice was softer than Shanna would have believed possible, but she had no time to wonder at it. Sleep enfolded her as the mist had muffled the moors while old Ama was still bidding her pleasant dreams.

And as if her words had been a spell, Shanna did dream – confused sequences from her wanderings all mixed in with scenes from her past that came and disappeared just as she was about to understand their significance. She saw her brother Janos as he had looked when he set out to offer fealty to the Emperor in Bindir, eyes glowing like a young god's. But there was something she had to tell him before he left Sharteyn – it was on the tip of her tongue, but before she could speak the scene had changed. Now she was kneeling in the mud beside her servant Hwilos, trying to stanch the blood that flowed from his chest and keep him from dying as the other men of her escort had died. He struggled to tell her something, but, again, before she could understand it, the scene had changed and she was alone in a dim wasteland where ghosts drifted aimlessly. She drifted with them, without home or companion or goal.

Again the dream changed. Shanna was still wandering in the waste, but now something was chasing after her. Faster and faster she ran, and still it came after with a great beating of black wings, until she woke with the perspiration beading her face and her heart thudding as loud as the beat of Calur's hooves.

Shanna fought off the blankets and sat up, breathing deeply. She was still shuddering. It was very quiet in the dark room. Outdoors she could hear the whisper of wind, and the thrice-repeated screech of a raven. Inside, nothing moved, and the only light came from the last coals of the fire. No – it was not quite the only light. As she looked around, Shanna saw a faint radiance shining from the staff that old Yod had left leaning beside the door.

Shanna's head felt as if someone had been using it for a drum; it reminded her painfully of the headache she had had after the first time she had drunk too much country beer. After her dreams, she could have sworn that she would never sleep again, but her eyes had the heaviness that comes of oversleeping, and the light filtering through the oiled leather that covered the window seemed very bright.

Ama's voice cut painfully through the fog that swirled where Shanna's brain should be.

'I want fresh rushes – fresh ones, mind you, and I'll know where you got them by the color and kind, Master Yod – so don't you go trying any tricks on me!'

'Oh aye, you're the mistress here, and I'm just to fetch and carry for you, is that it?' He had wrapped himself in a fuzzy grey cloak that flapped around him as he shook his arm.

Shanna hauled on her boots and got painfully to her feet.

'And wasn't it you who was just complaining that this place was turning to a pigsty and you wanted some order here? Make up your mind, old man, that is, if you mind's not become as empty of sense as your pate is of hair.' She turned on him, gesturing with her broom.

Shanna began to edge toward the door, her headache forgotten in a fervent hope that Epona, the horse-goddess, had been merciful and a night's rest had been enough to fit Calur for the road again.

'You flap-dugged hag!' the old man exclaimed, 'I'll bare-pate you, I'll stir your cauldron for you, see if I don't – ' He picked up his staff, and Shanna took advantage of his movement to slip through the door.

Shanna had cleaned out and examined Calur's hooves as well as she could when she stabled the mare the night before. In the dimming light she had not been able to find anything jammed in the hoof, and she hoped that perhaps the mare had only suffered from a stone bruise. But as she opened the door of the shed, Calur lifted her head and took an uneven step toward her and stood with her right foreleg hardly touching the ground. Her eyes were dull, and her coat seemed to have lost some of its shine.

With a sinking feeling in her stomach, Shanna went to the mare and knelt beside her, gently lifting the foot and tapping the sole and frog of the hoof with the heavy hilt of her dagger to test for tenderness. Suddenly Calur flinched, jerking her foot from the girl's grasp.

'Turds!' muttered Shanna. She picked up the foot again, reversing the dagger and gently scraping at the impacted mud that had looked like part of the inner hoof the night before. Now she could feel heat in the hoof and the fetlock too. She finished cleaning out the hoof and washed it, but still she could see nothing. If gravel had gotten up behind the hoof wall, she would have to wait for it to work its way out at the top where she could extract it. And she would need hot water to soak it, and cleansing herbs. She swore again, realizing that Ama probably had just the thing in her cupboard, and that she was going to have to ask the old woman's help and stay here while she treated the mare.

She saw that Calur had scarcely touched the grass she had given her the night before, and realized just how sick she must be. She swore again and went into the house.

'I will treat the mare.' Ama's words offered no room for argument. 'I have the herbs and the spells that will make them efficacious, but if I am to spend my day tending your mount, you must help me with my tasks.'

'Yes, of course,' said Shanna. The old woman had fed her a chewy porridge with stewed fruit and some kind of herb tea that almost succeeded in clearing her head, and things seemed much more encouraging than they had when she woke up that morning. 'What do you need?'

For a moment the beady eyes that stared into her own grew

luminous. 'More than you can give me, granddaughter, but enough for me to give you.' Then the dark eyes hardened. 'I must make up a special medicine for the mare. You will have to fetch water from the stream to fill my cauldron.'

She handed her a wooden bucket, and Shanna nodded. The bucket could hold two gallons, and the cauldron looked as if it would hold about ten. Surely five trips to the stream would be enough to fill it up. She set off almost at a run.

When she returned from her first trip down the hill, Ama was gone. Shanna sloshed the water into the cauldron and detoured to the stable to check on Calur. The mare's fetlock had been neatly poulticed, and although she still moved painfully, she seemed a little more comfortable. Shanna shook her head. Ama had lived up to her part of the bargain – she should get the rest of the water now. The mare butted her gently in the chest, and for a moment Shanna held her. Calur was all that was left of her old life – if any harm came to her, what would there be to remind her of who she had once been?

She went out then and made her way down to the stream for more water. But when she poured the water into the cauldron the second time, there was something odd about the sound. She turned back to look into it – the water seemed low, but she had not really noticed how high it had been after she poured the first bucketful in. Her stomach tightening with an anxiety she would not name, she turned back toward the stream.

When Shanna came back with the third bucketful, she set it down beside the cauldron and looked inside before pouring it in. The bottom of the great pot was black and bare. She looked around her. Ama was still gone, and there were no marks in the rushes to indicate that the cauldron had been moved. Even if the old woman could have budged the thing by herself, she could not have done it without disturbing them. There must be some explanation. There had to be. Very carefully, Shanna tipped the bucket over the side of the cauldron and let the water pour in.

It swirled down the curving sides, but instead of settling at the bottom, it continued to whirl, funneling the water through an invisible opening. Around and around – her gaze followed it until it dizzied her. And then, with a last gurgle, it was gone.

No – she shook her head. That couldn't be. She reached down to touch the bottom, and it was hard and cold. Her throat closed and began to ache as she stared uncomprehending.

She had done what the old woman asked of her – she had poured the water into the cauldron – but there was nothing there! It was like her life, she thought dully. By now she should have been on her way back from the Emperor's court in Bindir as she had promised her father, with her brother by her side. That had seemed a worthy goal, but a year had passed and Bindir was still far away. If she had stayed with Lord Roalt, they would probably have been married by now, maybe with a child on the way. But instead she had nothing – nothing! All her labours had been as fruitless as her attempt to fill the cauldron.

But the cauldron must be filled, or Ama would not be able to brew her medicines, and Calur would die.

Tears stung her eyelids, but her eyes remained dry. She stared at the cauldron emptily.

'Weep – ' said a soft voice behind her. She turned and saw Yod, leaning on his staff. The evening before he had seemed faintly comic, but there was nothing funny about him now.

'I cannot weep,' she answered him. 'I have to be strong.'

'Weep,' he repeated. 'Even the strongest tree will crack if its roots get no nourishment.'

'No.' she said. 'I am a princess of Sharteyn . . . '

'Let the tears flow,' he told her. 'Are you too proud to share the common griefs of the children of men?'

And as if the images were flowing directly from his mind into hers, she saw a child weeping beside the body of her mother; tears of rage in the eyes of a farmer who watched warring armies trample his fields; the desolation of a lover bidding her beloved farewell. With a clarity she had not known for years, she remembered her own mother's funeral, and the uncomprehending grief of the child she had been. And finally she saw

Calur's hanging head and dull eyes, and her heart ached with a sense of impending loss.

Her eyes smarted like open wounds, and suddenly the tears began to fall, leaving shining trails down the curving sides of the cauldron and pooling in the bottom. Far more quickly than seemed possible, they covered it. The water rose until she could see her own face darkly mirrored, strong bones sharply defined by months of hard living, brown eyes which had not entirely lost their vulnerability. And still she wept, until the cauldron was filled.

'Taste it,' said Yod.

She stared at him. 'It will be salty.'

He offered her the dipper, and she slipped it beneath the shining surface of the liquid in the cauldron, then lifted and sipped carefully.

It was sweet, but when she turned to tell Yod, he was gone.

The next morning, Ama informed Shanna that in order to make new bandages for Calur's foot, she would need to spin more wool.

'On the moor Yod's sheep are grazing,' she said. 'Get a bagful of their wool and bring it here to me.'

Shanna nodded warily. She had seen it done, the protesting sheep viced by the shepherd's legs while he pulled out great handfuls of long-fibred, strong-smelling wool. It did not look hard, but she had spent too much of the night lying still in her blankets, trying to understand what was happening to her here, and she still did not know. She met Ama's gaze, but the black eyes were as opaque and uncommunicative as stones.

When Shanna came out of the cottage, she saw that swaths of mist lay in the slopes and hollows like wisps of wool and smiled at the analogy. Ama had said she would find the sheep on the hill above the house where the summer's warmth had cured the wild grass to hay. Wishing she had repaired her boot the night before.

Shanna slung the hemp bag over her shoulder and began to climb.

She sighed with relief when she found the flock, clumped at one end of the field as if the clouds had left dirty tatters stuck to the heather as they went by. She started across the slope. The sheep lifted their heads, looked at her suspiciously, and drifted farther up the hill. She stopped with a sigh. They regarded her for a moment longer, and then began to bite the tough grass once more.

A familiar feeling of frustration began to curdle in Shanna's belly as every move she made sent the sheep farther away. She tried to get up the slope above them, so that at least she would be driving them downhill, but when she got there half of them had somehow moved even farther above her. And the gray fleeces of those below blended with the fog that still clung to the hollows so that they were almost impossible to see.

I need a dog, or Chai! she thought angrily. But she had left the falcon in the house with Ama. She realized now that this was another test. She did not know why the old woman was setting it for her, but she believed that the life of her horse depended on whether or not she passed. Her thought continued, *I am still lost! If only I could understand!*

She searched the hillside desperately, and as her eyes passed the crest for a second time she saw Yod looking down at her, as still as any standing stone. Shanna raised her hand in salute to him.

'Master Yod, can you help me? I must catch the sheep to get wool for your old woman, and they won't stay still.'

'Will a drifting cloud stay still?' he asked as he moved down the hill toward her. 'If you cannot pluck them, you must let them pluck themselves.' He gestured toward the fold in the slope where a little stream carried the runoff from the moor. 'See, there they are – '

Shanna saw the sheep drinking with their feet in the water. She nodded and picked her way carefully through the heather. When she got to the stream the sheep were gone, but with a lightening at the heart she saw what Yod had meant, for where they had passed, the tufts and streamers of grey wool caught in the wiry branches fluttered in the little breeze. She opened the bag and began to harvest it.

Ama was spinning. Like magic, the swift twirling of the old woman's gnarled fingers transformed the cloudy wool into a strong thread. As the thread lengthened, the drop-spindle swung hypnotically. Shanna realized that she was staring, and forced her gaze back to the fire.

A small pot hung from the iron bracket in the hearth. She could smell the acrid odor of the herbs that were simmering there. If all went well, Calur's new medicine would be ready by morning. Already the mare's foot was improving – the new stuff should have her ready to travel soon.

'*Keep up the fire. You must keep it burning steadily. That is all you have to do.*' Ama had said to her. Shanna peered under the round base of the pot and reached for another stick to feed the flames. Across the room, Yod sat in his great chair, making notes in the margins of a tattered roll of manuscript that rested upon his knees. For once, the two of them had stopped their bickering. The scratching of his quill on the parchment blended into the whisper of the fire.

Ama hummed steadily as she spun, the sound as mesmerizing as the movement of her hands. Shanna found her vision blurring and shook her head to clear it. In the dry warmth of the fire it was hard to remember Calur's danger and her own despair. She stared into glowing caverns of flame, following their windings . . .

'Child – are you asleep there? Look to the fire!'

Shanna jerked upright, blinking. The room was suddenly very dark. Had she been sleeping? Frantic, she snatched fuel from the basket and thrust it into the hearth.

The fire blazed up as if something more flammable than wood had been hidden in the fuel, hiding the pot and billowing out into the room. Chai exploded from her place on the mantel in a flurry of wings. Instinctively, Shanna grabbed her cloak and began to beat at the flames, but the flapping only served to fan them.

And as she struggled, she saw suddenly a darkly shining figure lift a sword of flame. She dropped her cloak and snatched her own blade from the wall, yanking it from the sheath as the fiery warrior darted toward her.

And then she had her sword free. Her blade came up, she settled into the balanced fighting stance that practice with Lord Roalt had grafted onto the training her brother's swordmaster had given her. Her heart flamed with exultation – at last there was something to fight, a way to strike at all the frustration and uncertainty!

Her sword seemed to move of itself as she turned, back and around in a smooth cut toward the shrouded head behind that glowing blade. But it was the opposing blade that it touched, and as the two weapons clashed, fire ran from her enemy's sword down her own and flared through her.

Pain! She had forgotten what pain could be! She struggled to get up and keep battling. But her nerves were still paralyzed. As she lay gasping, a still voice whispered in her ear –

'This is not an enemy you can overcome by fighting – give yourself to the flames!'

With every nerve twitching, Shanna managed to push herself up on her hands and knees. Her sword was still in her hand. She looked up, trying to penetrate the veil of flame that hid her opponent. As she had not known how to weep, she did not know how to surrender. She could only remember how she had given herself to the dance of death in the fight in which she won her sword.

Dimly she understood that this was a test, too. *For Calur* – she said into her heart's confusion, *to save Calur!*

With a sigh, she sat back on her heels, brought up her blade in a salute, and then very deliberately opened her guard.

The flaming blade came down, searing every nerve with ecstasy; flame billowed around her like a bright cloak opening.

And behind that radiance she saw a woman's form, and a face with eyes that shone like twin stars.

'*My Daughter*', a voice spoke in her soul, '*Why are you fighting Me?*'

Shanna lifted her hands in homage, and her greeting was a prayer –

'Yraine . . . '

As she spoke the name of the Goddess, darkness reversed the light. Shanna blinked, trying to recover her vision. When she could see again she found that not only the light, but the cottage and all it contained had disappeared. The moor stretched away to every side, veiled in ground-mist, but a cold wind was blowing, revealing the stars. She found her cloak beside her and, shivering, pulled it on.

Then she heard the musical 'keaar, keaar' of a falcon's cry and, looking up, saw Chai's elegant silhouette against the stars. The falcon circled above her and soared ahead. Shanna got to her feet and, still holding her drawn sword, followed her.

In that dim waste she could not tell how far she walked, for she did not feel tired. She was not even sure it was the common earth she trod, for despite the lack of light she did not stumble. She did not know where she was going, or where she had been, she only knew that as long as Chai flew forward, she had to go after her.

The ground began to rise, and a jumble of stones loomed through the mist. Chai cried out and swooped downwards as Shanna climbed toward them. Then she stoped, startled, for the shapes before her were not all stone. Someone was sitting there. With a tightening of the nerves, she recognized the old woman and the old man of the cottage.

'Master Yod, Mistress Ama – what are you doing here?'

There was a long silence, and Shanna felt cold fingers brush her spine.

'You will know that when you know who we are . . .'

This was another puzzle, like the tests the old woman had set her during the past three days. How could Shanna expect to know them by any names except those they had given her?

'Who are you?' The words pushed past her caution.

'Look at us and see – '

The wind's whisper echoed the word, an infinity of 'see,' 'see,' 'see,' rustling through the heather. Startled, Shanna looked around her, then back at the old woman and man who were regarding her so steadily. She had been telling herself that this must be some dream. But what if the world she had thought she was living in was the dream, and this the true reality? She blinked, trying to change her vision, but the dark world around her remained the same.

'I'm tired of riddles with no answers and games I never asked to play!' she exclaimed. 'Now you answer me! Why couldn't I fill the cauldron?'

'How could you have expected to? The cauldron holds all the waters of the sea.'

'Then what about the sheep?' Why were they so hard to catch?'

'Have you ever tried to catch a cloud?' It sounded like the old man's voice this time.

'And the fire?' she said then.

'The fire is the gift of the sun, to serve, or to slay. Some powers must not be mastered, but understood.'

Shanna nodded and, straightening, brought up her sword. 'My Goddess sent me to you. Who are you?'

The wind rushed around her in a confusion of voices, but Shanna could not concentrate on what they said, for her vision was altering, or perhaps it was the figures before her that were growing, until they towered like pillars toward the stars.

And as they expanded, they changed. The old woman's skin smoothed and her body firmed until she glowed with a terrible beauty, and the colour of her worn robes deepened to the black of the sea on a night without stars. She was hooded, and for that Shanna was grateful, for she knew that if she had been able to see that face fully she would have died of fear.

She turned quickly to the man, but the purity of his countenance was in its own way almost as fearful as the woman's implacable beauty. His beard shone like silver, and his rippling robes shone with the same pale radiance she had seen in his staff.

'You perceive us, mortal, in such fashion as your eyes can see. Are you answered?' The voice seemed to come from everywhere.

'I am answered,' she found the courage to say.

'Then you shall tell us what you are doing here, and what you desire.'

From some deep place within her, the words of the ritual came to Shanna then –

> *I am lost, and I would find my way.*
> *I am hungry, and I would be fed.*
> *I am dying, and I would be reborn . . .'*

And that was the truth of it, she understood then. She had lost all direction in her wanderings. It was not the mist on the moor that was imprisoning her, but the confusion in her own heart.

'As your spirit has spoken so it shall be.' came the answer. 'You have answered the questions, and passed the tests. Your road will never be easy, but when you know what you are truly seeking, it will be found.'

The radiance increased, dark and light, and the air rang.

I'm looking for my brother, came the automatic response. Then Shanna stopped herself – was that truly the answer? Her spirit quested inward, seeking truth, and the faces before her fused with the face she had seen in the fire, then changed to a Glory too great for her consciousness to apprehend.

And then the scene around her was dissolving. She felt herself falling, and knew no more.

Shanna woke still grasping at the skirts of a dream in which she had understood the meaning of all her pain. Dawn was turning the mists to veils of rose-gold, and she lay wrapped in her cloak beside the embers of a campfire upon the open moor. The details of

Shanna's dream faded swiftly, but the sense of a friendly presence glowing like a flame in the darkness, and the peace with which it had filled her, remained.

She was still alone in the wilderness, but she no longer felt the desperation that had driven her – no doubt she would have more battles to fight on her journey, but she need not fight the world as well. Shanna sat up, surprised that after such a night she was not stiff and sore, and looked around her.

She could not remember having made camp, but her gear was laid out beneath a weathered standing stone that overlooked a dark pool. Calur was drinking from it, her muzzle trailing ripples through the black waters. Calur! The mare had been in the dream too – there had been something wrong – with a low cry, Shanna reached out to her.

Seeing the girl's movement, the mare lifted her head and moved easily around the pool to butt her soft nose against Shanna's outstretched hand, and for a moment both horse and girl were outlined in gold by the light of the rising sun.

The Smallest Dragonboy

Anne McCaffrey

Many societies have rites of passage in which adolescents must complete certain ceremonial tasks before being considered adults or being allowed to assume adult responsibilities. On the strange world of Pern, for example, a young man cannot become a full-fledged dragonrider unless he is chosen from among many boys by one of Pern's telepathic dragons. But sometimes, even getting the chance to be chosen can be difficult.

Although Keevan lengthened his walking stride as far as his legs would stretch, he couldn't keep up with the other candidates. He knew he would be teased again.

Just as he knew many other things that his foster mother told him he ought not to know, Keevan knew that Beterli, the most senior of the boys, set that spanking pace just to embarrass him, the smallest dragonboy. Keevan would arrive, tail fork-end of the group, breathless, chest heaving, and maybe get a stern look from the instructing wingsecond.

Dragonriders, even if they were still only hopeful candidates for the glowing eggs which were hardening on the hot sands of the Hatching Ground cavern, were expected to be punctual and prepared. Sloth was not tolerated by the Weyrleader of Benden Weyr. A good record was especially important now. It was very near hatching time, when the baby dragons would crack their mottled shells, and stagger forth to choose their lifetime companions. The very thought of that glorious moment made Keevan's breath catch in his throat. To be chosen – to be a dragonrider! To sit astride the neck of a winged beast with jewelled eyes: to be his friend, in telepathic communion with him for life, to be his companion in good times and fighting extremes, to fly effortlessly over the lands of Pern! Or, thrillingly, *between* to any point anywhere on the world! Flying *between* was done on dragonback or not at all, and it was dangerous.

Keevan glanced upward, past the black mouths of the weyr caves in which grown dragons and their chosen riders lived, toward the Star Stones that crowned the ridge of the old volcano that was Benden Weyr. On the height, the blue watch dragon, his rider mounted on his neck, stretched the great transparent pinions that carried him on the winds of Pern to fight the evil Thread that fell at certain times from the skies. The many-faceted rainbow jewels of his eyes glistened fleetingly in the greeny sun. He folded his great wings to his back, and the watch pair resumed their statuelike pose of alertness.

Then the enticing view was obscured as Keevan passed into the Hatching Ground cavern. The sands underfoot were hot, even through heavy wher-hide boots. How the bootmaker had protested having to sew so small! Keevan was forced to wonder why being small was reprehensible. People were always calling him 'babe' and shooing him away as being 'too small' or 'too young' for this or that. Keevan was constantly working, twice as hard as any other boy his age, to prove himself capable. What if his muscles weren't as big as Beterli's? They were just as hard. And if he couldn't overpower anyone in a wrestling match, he could outdistance everyone in a footrace.

'Maybe if you run fast enough,' Beterli had jeered on the occasion when Keevan had been goaded to boast of his swiftness, 'you could catch a dragon. That's the only way you'll make a dragonrider!'

'You just wait and see, Beterli, you just wait,' Keevan had replied. He would have liked to wipe the contemptuous smile from Beterli's face, but the guy didn't fight fair even when a wingsecond was watching. 'No one knows what Impresses a dragon!'

'They've got to be able fo *find* you first, babe!'

Yes, being the smallest candidate was not an enviable position. It was therefore imperative that Keevan Impress a dragon in his first hatching. That would wipe the smile off every face in the cavern and accord him the respect due any dragonrider, even the smallest one.

Besides, no one knew exactly what Impressed the baby dragons as they struggled from their shells in search of their lifetime partners.

'I like to believe that dragons see into a man's heart,' Keevan's foster mother, Mende, told him. 'If they find goodness, honesty, a flexible mind, patience, courage – and you've got that in quantity, dear Keevan – that's what dragons look for. I've seen many a well-grown lad left standing on the sands, Hatching Day, in favour of someone not so strong or tall or handsome. And if my memory serves me' – which it usually did: Mende knew every word of every Harper's tale worth telling, although Keevan did not interrupt her to say so – 'I don't believe that F'lar, our Weyrleader, was all that tall when bronze Mnementh chose him. And Mnementh was the only bronze dragon of that hatching.'

Dreams of Impressing a bronze were beyond Keevan's boldest reflections, although that goal dominated the thoughts of every other hopeful candidate. Green dragons were small and fast and more numerous. There was more prestige to Impressing a blue or brown than a green. Being practical, Keevan seldom dreamed as high as a big fighting brown, like Canth, F'nor's fine fellow, the biggest brown of all Pern. But to fly a bronze? Bronzes were almost as big as the queen, and only they took the air when a queen flew at mating time. A bronze rider could aspire to become a Weyrleader! Well, Keevan would console himself, brown riders could aspire to become wing-seconds, and that wasn't bad. He'd even settle for a green dragon: they were small, but so was he. No matter! He simply had to Impress a dragon his first time in the Hatching Ground. Then no one in the Weyr would taunt him anymore for being so small.

Shells, Keevan thought now, but the sands are hot!

'Impression time is imminent, candidates,' the wingsecond was saying as everyone crowded respectfully close to him. 'See the extent of the striations on this promising egg.' The stretch marks *were* larger than yesterday.

Everyone leaned forward and nodded thoughtfully. That particular egg was the one Beterli had marked as his own, and no other candidate dared, on pain of being beaten by Beterli at his first opportunity, to approach it. The egg was marked by a large yellowish splotch in the shape of a dragon backwinging to land, talons outstretched to grasp rock. Everyone knew that bronze eggs bore distinctive markings. And naturally, Beterli, who'd been presented at eight Impressions already and was the biggest of the candidates, had chosen it.

'I'd say that the great opening day is almost upon us,' the wingsecond went on, and then his face assumed a grave expression. 'As we well know, there are only forty eggs and seventy-two candidates. Some of you may be disappointed on the great day. That doesn't mean you aren't dragonrider material, just that *the* dragon for you hasn't been shelled. You'll have other hatchings, and it's no disgrace to be left behind an Impression or two. Or more.'

Keevan was positive that the wingsecond's eyes rested on Beterli, who'd been stood off at so many Impressions already. Keevan tried to squinch down so that the wingsecond wouldn't notice him. Keevan had been reminded too often that he was eligible to be a candidate by one day only. He, of all the hopefuls, was most likely to be left standing on the great day. One more reason why he simply had to Impress at his first hatching.

'Now move about among the eggs,' the wingsecond said. 'Touch them. We don't know that it does any good, but it certainly doesn't do any harm.'

Some of the boys laughed nervously, but everyone immediately began to circulate among the eggs. Beterli stepped up officiously to 'his' egg, daring anyone to come near it. Keevan smiled, because he had already touched it – every inspection day, when the others were leaving the Hatching Ground and no one could see him crouch to stroke it.

Keevan had an egg he concentrated on, too, one drawn

slightly to the far side of the others. The shell had a soft greenish-blue tinge with a faint creamy swirl design. The consensus was that this egg contained a mere green, so Keevan was rarely bothered by rivals. He was somewhat perturbed then to see Beterli wandering over to him.

'I don't know why you're allowed in this Impression, Keevan. There are enough of us without a babe,' Beterli said, shaking his head.

'I'm of age,' Keevan kept his voice level, telling himself not to be bothered by mere words.

'Yah!' Beterli made a show of standing on his toetips. 'You can't even see over an egg; Hatching Day, you better get in front or the dragons won't see you at all. 'Course, you could get run down that way in the mad scramble. Oh, I forgot, you can run fast, can't you?'

'You'd better make sure a dragon sees *you*, this time, Beterli,' Keevan replied. 'You're almost overage, aren't you?'

Beterli flushed and took a step forward, hand half-raised. Keevan stood his ground, but if Beterli advanced one more step, he would call the wingsecond. No one fought on the Hatching Ground. Surely Beterli knew that much.

Fortunately, at that moment, the wingsecond called the boys together and led them from the Hatching Ground to start on evening chores. There were 'glows' to be replenished in the main kitchen caverns and sleeping cubicles, the major hallways, and the queen's apartment. Firestone sacks had to be filled against Thread attack, and black rock brought to the kitchen hearths. The boys fell to their chores, tantalized by the odours of roasting meat. The population of the Weyr began to assemble for the evening meal, and the dragonriders came in from the Feeding Ground on their sweep checks.

It was the time of day Keevan liked best: once the chores were done but before dinner was served, a fellow could often get close enough to the dragonriders to hear their talk, Tonight, Keevan's father, K'last, was at the main dragonrider table. It puzzled Keevan how his father, a brown rider and a tall man, could *be* his father – because he, Keevan, was so small. It obviously puzzled K'last, too, when he deigned to notice his small son: 'In a few more Turns, you'll be as tall as I am – or taller!'

K'last was pouring Benden wine all around the table. The dragonriders were relaxing. There'd be no Thread attack for three more days, and they'd be in the mood to tell tall tales, better than Harper yarns, about impossible manoeuvres they'd done a-dragonback. When Thread attack was closer, their talk would change to a discussion of tactics of evasion, of going *between*, how long to suspend there until the burning but fragile Thread would freeze and crack. And fall harmlessly off dragon and man. They would dispute the exact moment to feed firestone to the dragon so he'd have the best flame ready to sear Thread midair and render it harmless to ground – and man – below. There was such a lot to know and understand about being a dragonrider that sometimes Keevan was overwhelmed. How would he ever be able to remember everything he ought to know at the right moment? He couldn't dare ask such a question; this would only have given additional weight to the notion that he was too young yet to be a dragonrider.

'Having older candidates makes good sense,' L'vel was saying, as Keevan settled down near the table. 'Why waste four to five years of a dragon's fighting prime until his rider grows up enough to stand the rigours?' L'vel had Impressed a blue of Ramoth's first clutch. Most of the candidates thought L'vel was marvellous because he spoke up in front of the older riders, who awed them. 'That was well enough in the Interval when you didn't need to mount the full Weyr complement to fight Thread. But not now. Not with more eligible candidates than ever. Let the babes wait.'

'Any boy who is over twelve Turns has the right to stand in the Hatching Ground,' K'last replied, a slight smile on his face. He never argued or got angry. Keevan wished he were more like his father. And oh, how he wished he were a brown rider! 'Only a dragon – each particular dragon – knows what he wants in a rider. We certainly can't tell. Time and again the theorists,' K'last's smile deepened as he eyes swept those at the table, 'are surprised by dragon choice. *They* never seem to make mistakes, however.'

'Now, K'last, just look at the roster this Impression. Seventy-two boys and only forty eggs. Drop off the twelve youngest, and there's still a good field for the hatchlings to choose from. Shells! There are a couple of weyrlings unable to see over a wher egg much less a dragon! And years before they can ride Thread.'

'True enough, but the Weyr is scarcely under fighting strength, and if the youngest Impress, they'll be old enough to fight when the oldest of our current dragons go *between* from senility.'

'Half the Weyrbred lads have already been through several Impressions,' one of the bronze riders said then. 'I'd say drop some of *them* off this time. Give the untried a chance.'

'There's nothing wrong in presenting a clutch with as wide a choice as possible,' said the Weyrleader, who had joined the table with Lessa, the Weyrwoman.

'Has there ever been a case,' she said, smiling in her odd way at the riders, 'where a hatchling didn't choose?'

Her suggestion was almost heretical and drew astonished gasps from everyone, including the boys.

F'lar laughed. 'You say the most outrageous things, Lessa.'

'Well *has* there ever been a case where a dragon didn't choose?'

'Can't say as I recall one,' K'last replied.

'Then we continue in this tradition,' Lessa said firmly, as if that ended the matter.

But it didn't. The argument ranged from one table to the other all through dinner, with some favouring a weeding out of the candidates to the most likely, lopping off those who were very young or who had had multiple opportunities to Impress. All the candidates were in a swivet, though such a departure from tradition would be to the advantage of many. As the evening progressed, more riders were favouring eliminating the youngest and those who'd passed four or more Impressions unchosen. Keevan felt he could bear such a dictum only if Beterli were also eliminated. But this seemed less likely than that Keevan would be turfed out, since the Weyr's need was for fighting dragons and riders.

By the time the evening meal was over, no decision had been reached, although the Weyrleader had promised to give the matter due consideration.

He might have slept on the problem, but few of the candidates did. Tempers were uncertain in the sleeping caverns next morning as the boys were routed out of their beds to carry water and black rock and cover the 'glows.' Twice Mende had to call Keevan to order for clumsiness.

'Whatever is the matter with you, boy?' she demanded in exasperation when he tipped black rock short of the bin and sooted up the hearth.

'They're going to keep me from this Impression.'

'What?' Mende stared at him. 'Who?'

'You heard them talking at dinner last night. They're going to turf the babes from the hatching.'

Mende regarded him a moment longer before touching his arm gently. 'There's lots of talk around a supper table, Keevan. And it cools as soon as the supper. I've heard the same nonsense before every hatching, but nothing is ever changed.'

'There's always a first time,' Keevan answered, copying one of her own phrases.

'That'll be enough of that, Keevan. Finish your job. If the clutch does hatch today, we'll need full rock bins for the feast, and you won't be around to do the filling. All my fosterlings make dragonriders.'

'The first time?' Keevan was bold enough to ask as he scooted off with the rockbarrow.

Perhaps, Keevan thought later, if he hadn't been on that chore just when Beterli was also fetching black rock, things might have turned out differently. But he had dutifully trundled the barrow to the outdoor bunker for another load just as Beterli arrived on a similar errand.

'Heard the news, babe?' Beterli asked. He was grinning from ear to ear, and he put an unnecessary emphasis on the final insulting word.

'The eggs are cracking?' Keevan all but dropped the loaded shovel. Several anxieties flicked through his mind then: he was black with rock dust – would he have time to wash before donning the white tunic of candidacy? And if the eggs were hatching, why hadn't the candidates been recalled by the wingsecond?

'Naw! Guess again!' Beterli was much too pleased with himself.

With a sinking heart, Keevan knew what the news must be, and he could only stare with intense desolation at the older boy.

'C'mon! Guess, babe!'

'I've no time for guessing games,' Keevan managed to say with indifference. He began to shovel black rock into the barrow as fast as he could.

'I said, guess.' Beterli grabbed the shovel.

'And I said I have no time for guessing games.'

Beterli wrenched the shovel from Keevan's hands. 'Guess!'

'I'll have that shovel back, Beterli.' Keevan straightened up, but he didn't come to Beterli's bulky shoulder. From somewhere, other boys appeared, with barrows, some mysteriously alerted to the prospect of a confrontation among their numbers.

'Babes don't give orders to candidates around here, babe!'

Someone sniggered and Keevan, incredulous, knew that he must've been dropped from the candidacy.

He yanked the shovel from Beterli's loosened grasp. Snarling, the older boy tried to regain possession, but Keevan clung with all his strength to the handle, dragged back and forth as the stronger boy jerked the shovel about.

With a sudden, unexpected movement, Beterli rammed the handle into Keevan's chest, knocking him over the barrow handles. Keevan felt a sharp, painful jab behind his left ear, an unbearable pain in his left shin, and then a painless nothingness.

Mende's angry voice roused him, and startled, he tried to throw back the covers, thinking he'd overslept. But he couldn't move, so firmly was he tucked into his bed. And then the constriction of a bandage on his head and the dull sickishness in his leg brought back recent occurrences.

'Hatching?' he cried.

'No, lovey,' Mende said in a kind voice. Her hand was cool and gentle on his forehead. 'Though there's some as won't be at any hatching again.' Her voice took on a stern edge.

Keevan looked beyond her to see the Weyrwoman, who was frowning with irritation.

'Keevan, will you tell me what occurred at the black-rock bunker?' asked Lessa in an even voice.

He remembered Beterli now and the quarrel over the shovel and . . . what had Mende said about some not being at any hatching? Much as he hated Beterli, he couldn't bring himself to tattle on Beterli and force him out of candidacy.

'Come, lad,' and a note of impatience crept into the Weyrwoman's voice. 'I merely want to know what happened from you too. Mende said she sent you for black rock. Beterli – and every Weyrling in the cavern – seems to have been on the same errand. What happened?

'Beterli took my shovel. I hadn't finished with it.'

'There's more than one shovel. What did he *say* to you?'

'He'd heard the news.'

'What news?' The Weyrwoman was suddenly amused.

'That . . . that . . . there'd been changes?'

'Is that what he said?'

'Not exactly.'

'What did he say? C'mon, lad, I've heard from everyone else, you know.'

'He said for me to guess the news.'

'And you fell for that old gag?' The Weyrwoman's irritation returned.

'Consider all the talk last night at supper, Lessa,' Mende said. 'Of course the boy would think he'd been eliminated.'

'In effect, he is, with a broken skull and leg.' Lessa touched his arm in a rare gesture of sympathy. 'Be that as it may, Keevan, you'll have other Impressions. Beterli will not. There are certain rules that must be observed by all candidates, and his conduct proves him unacceptable to the Weyr.'

She smiled at Mende and then left.

'I'm still a candidate?' Keevan asked urgently.

'Well, you are and you aren't, lovey,' his foster mother said. 'Is the numbweed working?' she asked, and when he nodded, she said, 'You just rest. I'll bring you some nice broth.'

At any other time in his life, Keevan would have relished such cosseting, but now he just lay there worrying. Beterli had been dismissed. Would the others think it was his fault? But everyone was there! Beterli had provoked that fight. His worry increased, because although he heard excited comings and goings in the passageway, no one tweaked back the curtain across the sleeping alcove he shared with five other boys. Surely one of them would have to come in sometime. No, they were all avoiding him. And something else was wrong. Only he didn't know what.

Mende returned with broth and beachberry bread.

'Why doesn't anyone come to see me, Mende? I haven't done anything wrong, have I? I didn't ask to have Beterli turfed out.'

Mende soothed him, saying everyone was busy with noon-time chores and no one was angry with him. They were giving him a chance to rest in quiet. The numbweed made him drowsy, and her words were fair enough. He permitted his fears to dissipate. Until he heard a hum. Actually, he felt it first, in the broken shin bone and his sore head. The hum began to grow. Two things registered suddenly in Keevan's groggy mind: the only white candidate's robe still in the pegs in the chamber was his; and the dragons hummed when a clutch was being laid or being hatched. Impression! And he was flat abed.

Bitter, bitter disappointment turned the warm broth sour in his belly. Even the small voice telling him that he'd have other opportunities failed to alleviate his crushing depression. *This* was the Impression that mattered! This was his chance to show *everyone*, from Mende to K'last to L'vel and even the Weyrleader that he, Keevan, was worthy of being a dragonrider.

He twisted in bed, fighting against the tears that threatened to choke him. Dragonmen don't cry! Dragonmen learn to live with pain.

Pain? The leg didn't actually pain him as he rolled about on his bedding. His head felt sort of stiff from the tightness of the bandage. He sat up, an effort in itself since the numbweed made exertion difficult. He touched the splinted leg; the knee was unhampered. He had no feeling in his bone, really. He swung himself carefully to the side of his bed and stood slowly. The room wanted to swim about him. He closed his eyes, which made the dizziness worse, and he had to clutch the wall.

Gingerly, he took a step. The broken leg dragged. It hurt in spite of the numbweed, but what was pain to a dragonman?

No one had said he couldn't go to the Impression. 'You are and you aren't,' were Mende's exact words.

Clinging to the wall, he jerked off his bedshirt. Stretching his arm to the utmost, he jerked his white candidate's tunic from the peg. Jamming first one arm and then the other into the holes, he pulled it over his head. Too bad about the belt. He couldn't wait. He hobbled to the door, hung on to the curtain to steady himself. The weight on his leg was unwieldy. He wouldn't get very far without something to lean on. Down by the bathing pool was one of the long crook-necked poles used to retrieve clothes from the hot washing troughs. But it was down there, and he was on the level above. And there was no one nearby to come to his aid: everyone would be in the Hatching Ground right now, eagerly waiting for the first egg to crack.

The humming increased in volume and tempo, an urgency to which Keevan responded, knowing that his time was all too limited if he was to join the ranks of the hopeful boys standing around the cracking eggs. But if he hurried down the ramp, he'd fall flat on his face.

He could, of course, go flat on his rear end, the way crawling children did. He sat down, sending a jarring stab of pain through his leg and up to the wound on the back of his head. Gritting his teeth and blinking away tears, Keevan scrabbled down the ramp. He had to wait a moment at the bottom to catch his breath. He got to one knee, the injured leg straight out in front of him. Somehow, he managed to push himself erect, though the room seemed about to tip over his ears. It wasn't far to the crooked stick, but it seemed an age before he had it in his hand.

Then the humming stopped!

Keevan cried out and began to hobble frantically across the cavern, out to the bowl of the Weyr. Never had the distance between living caverns and the Hatching Ground seemed so great. Never had the Weyr been so breathlessly silent. It was as if the multitude of people and dragons watching the hatching held every breath in suspense. Not even the wind muttered down the steep sides of the bowl. The only sounds to break the stillness were Keevan's ragged gasps and the thump-thud of his stick on the hard-packed ground. Sometimes he had to hop twice on his good leg to maintain his balance. Twice he fell into the sand and had to pull himself up on the stick, his white tunic no longer spotless. Once he jarred himself so badly he couldn't get up immediately.

Then he heard the first exhalation of the crowd, the oohs, the muted cheer, the susurrus of excited whispers. An egg had cracked, and the dragon had chosen his rider. Desperation increased Keevan's hobble. Would he never reach the arching mouth of the Hatching Ground?

Another cheer and an excited spate of applause spurred Keevan to greater effort. If he didn't get there in moments, there'd be no unpaired hatchling left. Then he was actually staggering into the Hatching Ground, the sands hot on his bare feet.

No one noticed his entrance or his halting progress. And Keevan could see nothing but the backs of the white-robed candidates, seventy of them ringing the area around the eggs.

Then one side would surge forward or back and there'd be a cheer. Another dragon had been Impressed. Suddenly a large gap appeared in the white human wall, and Keevan had his first sight of the eggs. There didn't seem to be *any* left uncracked, and he could see the lucky boys standing beside wobble-legged dragons. He could hear the unmistakable plaintive crooning of hatchlings and their squawks of protest as they'd fall awkwardly in the sand.

Suddenly he wished that he hadn't left his bed, that he'd stayed away from the Hatching Ground. Now everyone would see his ignominious failure. So he scrambled as desperately to reach the shadowy walls of the Hatching Ground as he had struggled to cross the bowl. He mustn't be seen.

He didn't notice, therefore, that the shifting group of boys remaining had begun to drift in his direction. The hard pace he had set himself and his cruel disappointment took their double toll of Keevan. He tripped and collapsed sobbing to the warm sands. He didn't see the consternation in the watching Weyrfolk above the Hatching Ground, nor did he hear the excited whispers of speculation. He didn't know that the Weyrleader and Weyrwoman had dropped to the arena and were making their way toward the knot of boys slowly moving in the direction of the entrance.

'Never seen anything like it,' the Weyrleader was saying. 'Only thirty-nine riders chosen. And the bronze trying to leave the Hatching Ground without making Impression.'

'A case in point of what I said last night,' the Weyrwoman replied, 'where a hatchling makes no choice because the right boy isn't there.'

'There's only Beterli and K'last's young one missing. And there's a full wing of likely boys to choose from . . .'

'None aceptable, apparently. Where is the creature going? He's not heading for the entrance after all. Oh, what have we there, in the shadows?'

Keevan heard with dismay the sound of voices nearing him.

He tried to burrow into the sand. The mere thought of how he would be teased and taunted now was unbearable.

Don't worry! Please don't worry! The thought was urgent, but not his own.

Someone had kicked sand over Keevan and butted roughly against him.

'Go away. Leave me alone!' he cried.

Why? was the injured-sounding question inserted into his mind. There was no voice, no tone, but the question was there, perfectly clear, in his head.

Incredulous, Keevan lifted his head and stared into the glowing jewelled eyes of a small bronze dragon. His wings were wet, the tips drooping in the sand. And he sagged in the middle on his unsteady legs, although he was making a great effort to keep erect.

Keevan dragged himself to his knees, oblivious of the pain in his leg. He wasn't even aware that he was ringed by the boys passed over, while thirty-one pairs of resentful eyes watched him Impress the dragon. The Weyrmen looked on, amused and surprised at the draconic choice, which could not be forced. Could not be questioned. Could not be changed.

Why? asked the dragon again. *Don't you like me?'* His eyes whirled with anxiety, and his tone was so piteous that Keevan staggered forward and threw his arms around the dragon's neck, stroking his eye ridges, patting the damp, soft hide, opening the fragile-looking wings to dry them, and wordlessly assuring the hatchling over and over again that he was the most perfect, most beautiful, most beloved dragon in the Weyr, in all the Weyrs of Pern.

'What's his hame, K'van?' asked Lessa, smiling warmly at the new dragonrider. K'van stared up at her for a long moment. Lessa would know as soon as he did. Lessa was the only person whou could 'receive' from all dragons, not only her own Ramoth. Then he gave her a radiant smile, recognizing the traditional shortening of his name that raised him forever to the rank of dragonrider.

My name is Heth, the dragon thought mildly, then hiccuped in sudden urgency. *I'm hungry.*

'Dragons are born hungry,' said Lessa laughing. 'F'lar, give the boy a hand. He can barely manage his own legs, much less a dragon's.'

K'van remembered his stick and drew himself up. 'We'll be just fine, thank you.'

'You may be the smallest dragonrider ever, young K'van,' F'lar said, 'but you're one of the bravest!'

And Heth agreed! Pride and joy so leaped in both chests that K'van wondered if his heart would burst right out of his body. He looped an arm around Heth's neck and the pair, the smallest dragonboy and the hatchling who wouldn't choose anybody else, walked out of the Hatching Ground together forever.

Kid Cardula

Jack Ritchie

It's just about time for me to close down the gym for the night when this tall stranger comes up to me.

He wears a black hat, black suit, black shoes, black topcoat, and he carries a zipper bag.

His eyes are black too. 'I understand that you manage boxers?'

I shrug. 'I had a few good boys in my time.'

Sure, I had a few good boys, but never *real* good. The best I ever done was with Chappie Strauss. He was listed as number ten in the lightweight division by *Ring Magazine*. Once. And I had to pick my fights careful to get him that far. Then he meets Galanio, which is a catastrophe, and he loses his next four fights too before I decide it's time to retire him.

'I would like you to manage me,' the stranger says. 'I plan to enter the fight ring.'

I look him over. He seems well built and I put his weight at around one-ninety. Height maybe six foot one. But he looks pale, like his face hasn't seen the sun for some time. And there is also the question of his age. It's hard to pin-point, but he's no kid.

'How old are you?' I ask.

He shifts a little. 'What is the ideal age for a boxer?'

'Mister,' I say, 'in this state it's illegal for any man over forty to even step into the ring.'

'I'm thirty,' he says fast. 'I'll see that you get a birth certificate to verify that.'

I smile a little. 'Look, man, at thirty in this game, you're just about over the hill. Not starting.'

His eyes glitter a little. 'But I am strong. Incredibly strong.'

I stretch the smile to a grin. 'Like the poet says, you got the strength of ten because your heart is pure?'

He nods. 'I do literally have the strength of ten, though not for that reason. As a matter of fact, realizing that I possesed this tremendous strength, it finally occurred to me that I might as well capitalize on it. Legitimately.'

He puts down the zipper bag and walks over to where a set of barbells is laying on the mat and does a fast clean and jerk like he was handling a baby's rattle.

I don't know how many pounds is on that bar, weight lifting not being my field. But I remember seeing Wisniewski working with those weights a couple of hours ago and he grunts and sweats and Wisniewski is a heavyweight with a couple of state lifting titles to his credit.

I'm a little impressed, but still not too interested. 'So you're strong. Maybe I can give you the names of a few of the weightmen who work out here. They got some kind of a club.'

He glares, at which he seems good. 'There is no money in weight lifting and I need a great deal of money.' He sighs. 'The subject of money never really entered my mind until recently. I simply dipped into my capital when necessary and then suddenly I woke one evening to discover that I was broke.'

I look him over again. His clothes look expensive, but a touch shabby, like they been worn too long and maybe slept in.

'I do read the newspapers,' he says, 'including the sports pages, and I see that there is a fortune to be made in the prize ring with a minimum of effort.' He indicates the zipper bag. 'Before I ran completely out of money, I bought boxing trunks and shoes. I will have to borrow the boxing gloves.'

I raise an eyebrow. 'You mean you want to step into the ring with somebody right now?'

'Precisely.'

I look down the gym floor. By now the place is empty except for Alfie Bogan, who's still working out on the heavy bag.

Alfie Bogan is a good kid and a hard worker. He's got a fair punch and high hopes for the ring. So far he's won all six of his fights, three by knockouts and three by decisions. But I can see what's in his future. He just don't have enough to get to the top.

All right, I think to myself. Why not give the gentleman in black a tryout and get this over with so I can get to bed, which is a cot in my office.

I call Alfie over and say, 'This here nice man wants to step into the ring with you for a couple of rounds.'

It's okay with Alfie, so the stranger disappears into the locker room and comes back wearing black trunks.

I fit him with gloves and he and Alfie climb into the ring and go to opposite corners.

I take the wrapper off a new cigar, stroke the gong, and start lighting up.

Alfie comes charging out of his corner, the way he always does, and meets the stranger three-quarters of the way across the ring. He throws a right and a left hook, which the stranger shrugs off. Then the stranger flicks out his left. You don't really see it, you just know it has happened. It connects with Alfie's chin and Alfie hits the canvas on his back and stays there. I mean he's out.

I notice that my match is burning my fingers and quick blow it out. Then I climb into the ring to look at Alfie. He's still breathing, but he won't be awake for a while.

When you been in the fight game as long as I have, you don't need no long study to rate a fighter. Just that one left – and even the *sound* of it connecting – has got my heart beating a little faster.

I look around the gym for somebody to replace Alfie, but like I said before, it's empty. I lick my lips. 'Kid, what about your right hand? Is it anywhere near as good as your left?'

'Actually my right hand is the better of the two.'

I begin to sweat with the possibilities. 'Kid, I'm impressed by your punch. I'll admit that. But the fight game is more than just punching. Can you *take* a punch too?'

He smiles thin – like a kid wearing new braces. 'Of course. Please hit me.'

Why not? I think. I might as well find out right now if he can take a punch. I take the glove off Alfie's right hand and slip into it.

In my day – which was thirty years ago – I had a pretty good right and I think I still got most of it. So I haul off and give it all I got. Right on the button of his chin.

And then I hop around the ring with tears in my eyes because I think I just busted my hand, but the stranger is still standing there with that narrow smile on his face and his hair not even mussed.

Alfie comes back into this world while I'm checking my hand and am relieved to discover that it ain't broken after all.

He groans and staggers to his feet, ready to start all over again. 'A lucky punch.' The boy is all heart, but no brains.

'No more tonight, Alfie,' I say. 'Some other time.' I send him off to the showers and take the stranger into my ofice. 'What's your name?'

'I am known as Cardula.'

Cardula? Probably Puerto Rican, I guess. He's got a little accent. 'All right,' I say, 'from now on you're Kid Cardula. Call me Manny.' I light my cigar. 'Kid, I just *may* be able to make something out of you. But first, let's get off on the right foot by making everything legal. First thing tomorrow morning we see my lawyer and he'll draw up papers which make us business associates.'

Kid Cardula looks uneasy. 'Unfortunately I can't make it tomorrow morning. Or the afternoon. For that matter, I can't make it *any* morning or afternoon.

I frown. 'Why not?'

'I suffer from what may be termed photophobia.'

'What's photophobia?'

'I simply cannot endure sunlight.'

'You break out in a rash or something?'

'Quite a bit more than a rash.'

I chew my cigar. 'Does this photophobia hurt your fighting any?'

'Not at all. Actually I regard it as responsible for my strength. However all of my matches will have to be scheduled for evenings.'

'Not much sweat there. Damn near all matches today are in the evening anyway.' I think a little while. 'Kid, I don't think we need to mention this photophobia to the State Medical Commission. I don't know how they stand on the subject and it's better we take no chances. This photophobia isn't catching, is it?'

'Not in the usual sense.' He smiles wide this time, and I see why he's been smiling tight before. He's got these two outsize upper teeth, one on each side of his mouth. Personally, if I had teeth like that, I'd have them pulled, whether they got cavities or not.

He clears his throat. 'Manny, would it be at all possible for me to get an advance on my future earnings?'

Ordinarily if anybody I just meet for the first time asks me for money, I tell him to forget it. But with Kid Cardula and his future, I think I can make an exception. 'Sure, Kid,' I say. 'I guess you're a little short on eating money?'

'I am not particularly concerned about eating money,' the Kid says. 'But my landlord threatens to evict me if I don't pay the rent.'

The next morning at around eleven, I get a phone call from Hanahan. It's about the McCardle-Jabloncic main event on Saturday night's card at the arena.

McCardle is Hanahan's pride and joy. He's a heavyweight, got some style and speed, and he's young. Hanahan is bringing him along careful, picking and choosing. Maybe McCardle isn't exactly championship material, but he should get in a few big money fights before it's time to retire.

'Manny,' Hanahan says, 'we got a little trouble with the Saturday night card. Jabloncic showed up at the weigh-ins with a virus, so he got scratched. I need somebody to fill in. You got anybody around there who'll fit the role?'

Jabloncic has 18 wins and 10 losses, which record don't look too bad on paper, except that it don't mention that he got six of them losses – all by knockouts – in a row after his eighteenth win. So I know exactly what type of fighter Hanahan wants as a substitute for Jabloncic.

I think a little. Off hand, there are three or four veterans who hang around the gym and could use the money and don't mind the beating.

And then I remember Kid Cardula.

Ordinarily when you got a new boy, you bring him up slow, like three-round preliminaries. But with Kid Cardula I feel I got something that can't wait and we might as well take some shortcuts.

I speak into the phone. 'Well, off-hand, Hanahan, I can't think of anybody except this new face that just come in to me last night. Kid Cardula, I think he calls himself.'

'Never heard of him. What's his win-lose?'

'I don't know. He's some kind of foreign fighter. Puerto Rico, I think. I don't have his records yet.'

Hanahan is cautious. 'You ever seen him fight?'

'Well, I put him in the ring here for just a few seconds to see if he has anything. His left is fair, but I never seen him use his right hand once. Don't even know if he has one.'

Hanahan is interested. 'Anything else?'

'He came in here wearing a shabby suit and gave me a sob story about being down and out. He's thirty-five if he's a day. I'll swear to that.'

Hanahan is pleased. 'Well, all right. But I don't want anybody *too* easy. Can he stand up for a couple of rounds?'

'Hanahan, I can't guarantee anything, but I'll try the best I can.'

That evening, when Kid Cardula shows up at the gym, I quick rush him to my lawyer and then to the weigh-in and physical under the arena, where I also sign papers which gives us ten percent of the night's gross.

I provide Kid Cardula with a robe which has got no lettering on the back yet, but it's black, his favourite colour, and we go out into the arena.

McCardle is a local boy, which means he's got a following. Half his neighbourhood is at the arena and it ain't really a bad house. Not like the old days, but good enough.

We set up shop inside the ring and when the bell rings, McCardle makes the sign of the cross and dances out of his corner.

But Kid Cardula don't move an inch. He turns to me, and his face looks scared. 'Does McCardle *have* to do that?'

'Do what?' I ask. 'Now look, Kid, this is no time to get stage fright. Get out there and fight.'

The Kid peeks back over his shoulder where the referee and McCardle are waiting for him in the centre of the ring. Then he takes a deep breath, turns, and glides out of our corner.

His left whips out, makes the connection with McCardle's jaw, and it's all over. Just like that. McCardle is lying there in the same pose as Alfie Bogan last night.

Even the referee is stunned and wastes a few seconds getting around to the count, not that it really matters. The bout is wrapped up in nineteen seconds, including the count.

There's some booing. Not because anybody thinks that McCardle threw the fight, but because everything went so quick with the wrong man winning and the fans figure they didn't get enough time for the price of their tickets.

When we're back in the dressing room, the first person who comes storming in is Hanahan, his face beet red. He glares at Kid Cardula and then drags me to a corner. 'What are you trying to do to me, Manny?'

I am innocence. 'Hanahan, I swear that was the luckiest punch I ever seen in my life.'

'You're damn right it was a lucky punch. We'll have the re-match as soon as I can book the arena again.'

'Re-match?' I rub my chin. 'Maybe so, Hanahan, but in this event I feel that I got to protect the Kid's interests. It's like a sacred trust. So for the re-match, we make his cut of the gate sixty percent instead of ten, right?'

Hanahan is fit to explode, but he's got this black spot on his fighter's record and the sooner he gets it off, the better. So by the time we finish yelling at each other, we decide to split the purse fifty-fifty, which is about what I expect anyway.

A couple of nights later when I close the gym and go to my office, I find the Kid sitting there watching the late show on my portable TV set. It's one of them Dracula pictures and he turns to another channel when I enter.

I nod. 'Never could stand them vampire pictures myself either. Even in a movie, I like logic, and they ain't got no logic.'

'No logic?'

'Right. Like when you start off with one vampire and he goes out and drinks somebody's blood and that turns his victim into a vampire too, right? So now there's *two* vampires. A week later, they both get hungry and go out and feed on two victims. Now you got *four* vampires. A week later them four vampires go out to feed and now you got *eight* vampires.'

'Ah, yes,' Kid Cardula says. 'And at the end of twenty-one weeks, one would logically expect to have a total of 1, 048, 576 vampires?'

'About that. And at the end of thirty weeks or so, everybody on the face of the earth is a vampire, and a week later all of them starve to death because they got no food supply anymore.'

Kid Cardula smiles, showing them big teeth. 'You've got a head on your shoulders, Manny. However, suppose that these fictitious vampires, realizing that draining *all* of the blood from their victims will turn them into vampires and thereby competitors, exercise a certain restraint instead? Suppose they simply take a sip, so to speak, from one person and a sip from the next, leaving their victims with just a slight anemia and lassitude for a few days, but otherwise none the worse for wear?'

I nod, turn down the TV volume and get back to the fight business. 'Now, Kid, I know that you'll be able to put McCardle away again in a few seconds, but we got to remember that fighting is also show biz. People don't pay good money for long to see twenty-second fights. We got to give the customers a performance that lasts a while. So when we meet McCardle again, I want you to carry him for a few rounds. Don't hit too hard. Make the match look even until say the fifth round and *then* put him away.'

I light a cigar. 'If we look too good, Kid, we'll have trouble getting opponents later and we got to think about the future. A string of knockouts is fine, Kid, but don't make them look too easy.'

In the weeks which follow while we're waiting for the McCardle re-match, I can't get the Kid to do any training at all – no road work and he won't even consider shadow boxing in front of a mirror.

So I leave it at that, not wanting to tamper with something that might be perfect. Also he won't give me his address. I suppose he's just got pride and don't want me to see the dump in which he lives. And he's got no phone. But he shows up at the gym every other night or so, just in case there's something concerning him.

The second McCardle fight comes and we take it in stride. The Kid carries McCardle for four rounds, but still making the bouts look good, and then in the fifth round he puts McCardle away with a short fast right.

In the days which follow, we don't have any particular trouble signing up more fights because we'll take any bout which comes our way. With Kid Cardula, I know I don't have to nurse him along. Also, we decide on the strategy of letting the Kid get himself knocked down two, maybe three, times per fight. With this manoeuvre, we establish that while the Kid can hit, he ain't so good at taking a punch. Consequently every manager who's got a pug with a punch figures that his boy has got a good chance of putting the Kid away.

We get seven bouts in the next year, all of which the Kid wins by knockouts, of course, and we're drawing attention from other parts of the country.

Now that some money is beginning to come in, I expect the Kid to brighten up a little, which he does for about six months, but then I notice that he's starting to brood about something. I try to get him to tell me about it, but he just shakes his head.

Also, now that he's getting publicity, he begins to attract the broads. They really go for his type. He's polite to them and all that, and even asks them their addresses, but as far as I know he never follows up or pays them a visit.

One morning after we'd just won our tenth fight – a nine round knockout over Irv Watson, who was on the way down, but still a draw – and I'm sitting in my office dreaming about the day soon when I sell the gym or at least hire somebody to manage it, there's a knock at the door.

The dame which enters and stands there looking scared is about your average height and weight, with average looks, and wearing good clothes. She's got black hair and a nose that's more than it should be. In all, nothing to get excited about.

She swallows hard. 'Is this where I can find Kid Cardula?'

'He drops in every now and then,' I say. 'But it's not a schedule. I never know when he'll turn up.'

'Would you have his address?'

'No. He likes to keep that a secret.'

She looks lost for a few seconds and then decides to tell me what brought her here. 'About two weeks ago, I drove out of state to see my aunt Harriet and when I came back, I got a late start and it got dark before I could make it home. I'm really not at all good with directions and it had been raining. I turned and turned, hoping that I'd find a road that looked familiar. Somehow I got on this muddy road and my car skidded right into a ditch. And I just couldn't get the car out. Finally I gave up and sat there, waiting for some car to pass, but there was no traffic at all. I couldn't even see a farmhouse light. I guess I finally fell asleep. I had the strangest dream, but I can't remember now exactly what it was, and when I woke, there was this tall distinguished looking man standing beside the open door of my car and staring down at me. He gave me quite a start at first, but I recovered and asked him if he'd give me a lift to someplace where I could get to a phone and call my father and have him send someone out to pick me up. His car was parked on the road and he drove me to a crossroads where there was a gas station open.'

I notice that she's got what look like two big mosquito bites on one side of her throat.

She goes on. 'Anyway, while I was making the phone call, he drove away before I could thank him or get his name. But I kept thinking about . . . ' She blushed. 'Then last night while I was watching the late news, there were things about sports and a picture of Kid Cardula appeared on the TV screen, and immediately I knew that his must be the stranger who had driven me to the gas station. So I asked around and somebody told me that you were his manager and gave me the address of your gym. And I just thought I'd drop in and thank him in person.'

I nod. 'I'll pass the thanks on to the Kid the next time I see him.'

She still stands there, thinking, and suddenly she brightens again. 'Also I wanted to return something to him. A money clip. With one thousand dollars in it. It was found beside my car when the tow truck went to pull it out of the ditch.'

Sure, I think. Some nice honest tow truck driver finds a thousand bucks on the ground and he doesn't put it in his own pocket. But I nod again. 'So give me the thousand and I'll see that the Kid gets it.'

She laughs a little. 'Unfortunately I forgot to bring the money and the clip with me.' She opens her purse and takes out a ball-point pen and some paper. 'My name is Carrington. Daphne Carrington. I'll write the directions on how to get to our place. It's a bit complicated. We call it Carrington Eyrie. Perhaps you've heard of it? It was featured in *Stately Home and Formal Garden Magazine* last year. Mr Cardula will have to come in person, of course. So that he can identify the clip.'

When Kid Cardula drops in the next evening, I tell him about Daphne Carrington and give him the slip of paper she left.

The Kid frowns. 'I didn't lose a thousand dollars. Besides, I never use a money clip.'

I grin. 'I thought not. But still she's willing to ante up a thousand bucks to meet you. Is any part of her story true?'

'Well . . . I *did* drive her to that filling station after I . . . after I found her asleep in the car.'

'I didn't know you owned a car.'

'I bought it last week. There are some places just too far to fly.'

'What model is it?'

'A 1974 Volkswagen. The motor's in good condition, but the body needs a little work.' He sits on the corner of my desk, his eyes thoughtful. '*She* was driving a Lincoln Continental.'

'Don't worry about it, Kid. Pretty soon you'll be driving Lincoln Continentals too.'

We begin spacing out our fights now. No bum-of-the-month stuff. Mostly because we're getting better quality opponents and also because it needs time and publicity to build up the interest and the big gates.

We win a couple more fights, which get television coverage, and the Kid should be happy, but he's still brooding.

And then one night he shows up in my office and he makes an announcement. 'Manny, I'm getting married.'

I'm a little astounded, but I see no threat. Lots of fighters are married. 'Who's the lucky lady?'

'Daphne Carrington.'

I think a while before the name connects. 'You mean *that* Daphne Carrington?'

He nods.

I stare at him. 'I hope you don't take this wrong, Kid, but the dame ain't exactly no Raquel Welch, even in the face department.'

His chin gets stubborn. 'She has a tremendous personality.'

That I doubt too. 'Kid,' I say, 'be honest with yourself. She just ain't your type.'

'She soon will be.'

Suddenly the nub of the situation seems to flash into my mind and I'm shocked. 'Kid you're not marrying this dame for her money, are you?'

He blushes, or looks like he tried to. 'Why not? It's been done before.'

'But, Kid, you don't *have* to marry anybody for their money. You're going to have money of your own soon. Big money. Millions.'

He looks away. 'Manny, I have been getting letters from my relatives and many concerned friends. But especially relatives. It seems that they have heard, or been told, about my ring appearances. And they all point out – rather strongly – that for a man with my background, it is unthinkable that I should be appearing in a prize ring.'

He still didn't look at me. 'I have been thinking this over for a long time, Manny, and I am afraid that they are right. I shouldn't be a boxer. Certainly not a professional. All of my family and all of my friends strongly disapprove. And, Manny, one must have one's own self-respect and the approval of one's peers if one wants to achieve any happiness in this world.'

'Peers?' I say. 'You mean like royalty? You a count or something? You got blue blood in your veins?'

'Occasionally.' He sighs. 'My relatives have even begun a collection to save me from destitution. But I cannot accept charity from relatives.'

'But you don't mind marrying a dame for her money?'

'My dear Manny,' he says. 'Marrying a woman for her money is as good a reason as any. Besides it will enable me to quit the fight game.'

We argue and argue and I beg him to think it over for a while, telling him what all that ring money could mean to him – and me.

Finally he seems to give in a little, and when he leaves, he at least promises to think it over for a while.

About a week passes. I don't hear from him and I'm a nervous wreck. Finally, at around ten-thirty one evening, Alfie Bogan comes into my office with an envelope.

Right away I get the feeling that the envelope should have a black border. My fingers tremble when I open it and read the note from Kid Cardula.

Dear Manny:

I sincerely regret the way things have turned out, but I am determined to quit the ring. I know that you pinned a great deal of hope on my future and I am certain that, under different circumstances, we would have made those millions you talked about.

But goodbye and good luck. I have, however, decided not to leave you empty handed.

Best wishes
Kid Cardula

Not leave me empty-handed? Did he enclose a nice little check? I shake the envelope, but nothing comes out. What did he mean he wouldn't leave me empty-handed.

I glare at Alfie Bogan, who's still standing there.

He grins. 'Hit me.'

I stare. Somehow Alfie looks different. He has two big mosquito bites on his throat and these two long upper teeth, which I swear I never seen before.

'Hit me,' he says again.

Maybe I shouldn't do it, but it's been a long hard week of disappointments. So I let him have it with all I got.

And break my hand.

But I'm smiling when the doc puts on the cast.

I got me a replacement for Kid Cardula.

The Green Road to Quephanda

Ruth Rendell

There used to be, not long ago, a London surburban line railway running up from Finsbury Park to Highgate, and further than that for all I know. They closed it down before I went to live at Highgate and at some point they took up the sleepers and the rails. But the track remains and a very strange and interesting track it is. There are people living in the vicinity of the old line who say they can still hear, at night and when the wind is right, the sound of a train pulling up the slope to Highgate and, before it comes into the old disused station, giving its long, melancholy, hooting call. A ghost train, presumably, on rails that have long been lifted and removed.

But this is not a ghost story. Who could conceive of the ghost, not of a person but of a place, and that place having no existence in the natural world? Who could suppose anything of a supernatural or paranormal kind happening to a man like myself, who am quite unimaginative and not observant at all?

An observant person, for instance, could hardly have lived for three years only two minutes from the old station without knowing of the existence of the line. Day after day, on my way to the Underground, I passed it, glanced down unseeing at the weed-grown platforms, the broken canopies. Where did I suppose those trees were growing, rowans and Spanish chestnuts and limes that drop their sticky black juice, like tar, that waved their branches in a long avenue high up in the air? What did I imagine that occasionally glimpsed valley was, lying between suburban back gardens? You may enter or leave the line at the bridges where there are always places for scrambling up or down, and at some actual steps, much overgrown, and gates or at least gateposts. I had been walking under or over those bridges (according as the streets where I walked passed under or over them) without ever asking myself what those bridges carried or crossed. It never even, I am sorry to say, occurred to me that there were rather a lot of bridges for a part of London where the only railway line, the Underground, ran deep in the bowels of the earth. I didn't think about them. As I walked under one of the brown brick tunnels I didn't look up to question its presence or ever once glance over a parapet. It was Arthur Kestrell who told me about the line, one evening while I was in his house.

Arthur was a novelist. I write 'was', not because he has abandoned his profession for some other, but because he is dead. I am not even sure whether one would call his books novels. They truly belong in that curious category, a fairly popular *genre*, that is an amalgam of science fiction, fairy tale and horror fantasy.

But Arthur, who used the pseudonym Blaise Fastnet, was no Mervyn Peake and no Lovecraft either. Not that I had read any of his books at the time of which I am writing. But Elizabeth, my wife, had. Arthur used sometimes to give us one of them on publication, duly inscribed and handed to us, presented indeed, with the air of something very precious and uniquely desirable being bestowed.

I couldn't bring myself to read them. The titles alone were enough to repel me: *Kallinarth, the Cloudling, The Quest of Kallinarth, Lord of Quephanda, The Grail-Seeker's Guerdon* and so forth. But I used somehow, without actually lying, to give Arthur the impression that I had read his latest, or I think I did. Perhaps, in fact, he saw through this, for he never enquired if I had enjoyed it or had any criticisms to make. Liz said they were 'fun', and sometimes – with kindly intent, I know – would refer to an incident or portion of dialogue in one of the books in Arthur's presence. 'As Kallinarth might have said,' she would say, or 'Weren't those the flowers Kallinarth picked for Valaquen when she woke from her long sleep?' This sort of thing only had the effect of making poor Arthur blush and look embarrassed. I believe that Arthur Kestrell was convinced in his heart that he was writing great literature, never perhaps to be recognized as such in his lifetime but for the appreciation of posterity. Liz, privately to me, used to call him the poor man's Tolkien.

He suffered from periods of black and profound depression. When these came upon him he couldn't write or read or even bring himself to go out on those marathon walks ranging across north London which he dearly loved when he was well. He would shut himself up in his Gothic house in that district where Highgate and Crouch End merge, and there he would hide and suffer and pace the floors, not answering the door, still less the telephone until, after five or six days or more, the mood of wretched despair had passed.

His books were never reviewed in the press. How it comes about that some authors' work never receives the attention of the critics is a mystery, but the implication, of course, is that it is beneath their notice. This ignoring of a new publication, this bland passing over with neither a smile nor a sneer, implies that the author's work is a mere commercially motivated repetition of his last book, a slight variation on a tried and lucrative theme, another stereotyped bubbler in a long line of profitable pot-boilers. Arthur, I believe, took it hard. Not that he told me so. But soon after Liz had scanned the papers for even a solitary line to announce a new Fastnet publication, one of these depressions of his would settle on him and he would go into hiding behind his grey, crenellated walls.

Emerging, he possessed for a while a kind of slow cheerfulness combined with a dogged attitude to life. It was always a pleasure to be with him, if for nothing else than the experience of his powerful and strange imagination whose vividness coloured those books of his, and in conversation gave an exotic slant to the observations he made and the opinions he uttered.

London, he always insisted, was a curious, glamorous and sinister city, hung on slopes and valleys in the north of the world. Did I not understand the charm it held for foreigners who thought of it with wistfulness as a grey Eldorado? I who had been born in it couldn't see its wonders, its contrasts, its wickednesses. In summer Arthur got me to walk with him to Marx's tomb, to the house where Housman wrote *A Shropshire Lad*, to the pond in the Vale of Health where Shelley sailed boats. We walked the Heath and we walked the urban woodlands and then one day, when I complained that there was nowhere left to go, Arthur told me about the track where the railway line had used to be. A long green lane, he said, like a country lane, four and a half miles of it, and smiling in his cautious way he told me where it went. Over Northwood Road, over Stanhope Road, under Crouch End Hill, over Vicarage Road, under Crouch Hill, under Mount View, over Mount Pleasant Villas, over Stapleton Hall, under Upper Tollington Park, over Oxford Road, under Stroud Green Road, and so to the station at Finsbury Park.

'How do you get on to it?' I said.

'At any of the bridges. Or at Holmesdale Road. You can get on to it from the end of my garden.'

'Right,' I said. 'Let's go. It's a lovely day.'

'There'll be crowds of people on a Saturday,' said Arthur. 'The sun will be bright like fire and there'll be hordes of wild people and their bounding dogs and their children with music machines and tinned drinks.' This was the way Arthur talked, the words juicily or dreamily enunciated. 'You want to go up there when it's quiet, at twilight, at dusk, when the air is lilac and you can smell the bitter scent of the tansy.'

'Tomorrow night then. I'll bring Liz and we'll call for you and you can take us up there.'

But on the following night when we called at Arthur's house and stood under the stone archway of the porch and rang his bell, there was no answer. I stepped back and looked up at the narrow latticed windows, shaped like inverted shields. This was something which, in these circumstances, I had never done before. Arthur's face looked back at me, blurred and made vague by the dark, diamond-paned glass, but unmistakably his small wizened face, pale and with its short, sparse beard. It is a disconcerting thing to be looked at like this by a dear friend who returns your smile and your mouthed greeting with a dead, blank and unrecognizing stare. I suppose I knew then that poor Arthur wasn't quite sane any more. Certainly Liz and I both knew that he had entered one of his depressions and that it was useless to expect him to let us in.

We went off home, abandoning the idea of an exploration of the track that evening. But on the following day, work being rather slack at that time of the year, I found myself leaving the office early and getting out of the tube train at Highgate at half-past four. Liz, I knew, would be out. On an impulse, I crossed the street and turned into Holmesdale Road. Many a time, walking there before, I had noticed what seemed an unexpectedly rural meadow lying to the north of the street, a meadow overshadowed by broad trees, though no more than fifty yards from the roar and stench of the Archway Road. Now I understood what it was. I walked down the slope, turned southeastwards where the meadow narrowed and came on to a grassy lane.

It was about the width of an English country lane and it was bordered by hedges of buddleia on which peacock and small tortoise-shell butterflies basked. And I might have felt myself truly in the country had it not been for the backs of houses glimpsed all the time between the long leaves and purple spires of the buddleia bushes. Arthur's lilac hour had not yet come. It was windless sunshine up on the broad green track, the clear, white light of a sun many hours yet from setting. But there was a wonderful warm and rural, or perhaps I should say pastoral, atmosphere about the place. I need Arthur's gift for words and Arthur's imagination to describe it properly and that I don't have. I can only say that there seemed, up there, to be a suspension of time and also of the hurrying, frenzied bustle, the rage to live, that I had just climbed up out of.

I went over the bridge at Northwood Road and over the bridge at Stanhope Road, feeling ashamed of myself for having so often walked unquestioningly *under* them. Soon the line began to descend, to become a valley rather than a causeway, with embankments on either side on which grew small, delicate birch trees and the rosebay willow herb and the giant hogweed. But there were no tansy flowers, as far as I could see. These are bright yellow double daisies borne in clusters on long stems and they have the same sort of smell as chrysanthemums. For all I know, they may be a sort of chrysanthemum or belonging to that family. Anyway, I couldn't see any or any lilac, but perhaps Arthur hadn't meant that and in any case it wouldn't be in bloom in July. I went as far as Crouch End Hill that first time and then I walked home by road. If I've given the impression there were no people on the line, this wasn't so. I passed a couple of women walking a labrador, two boys with bikes and a little girl in school uniform eating a choc ice.

Liz was intrigued to hear where I had been but rather cross that I hadn't waited until she could come too. So that evening, after we had had our meal, we walked along the line the way and the distance I had been earlier and the next night we ventured into the longer section. A tunnel blocked up with barbed wire prevented us from getting quite to the end but we covered nearly all of it and told each other we very likely hadn't missed much by this defeat.

The pastoral atmosphere disappeared after Crouch End Hill. Here there was an old station, the platforms alone still remaining, and under the bridge someone had dumped an old feather mattress – or plucked a dozen geese. The line became a rubbish dump for a hundred yards or so and then widened out into children's playgrounds with murals – and graffitti – on the old brick walls.

Liz looked back at the green valley behind. 'What you gain on the swings,' she said, 'you lose on the roundabouts.' A child in a rope seat swung past us, shrieking, nearly knocking us over.

All the prettiness and the atmosphere I have tried to describe was in that first section, Highgate station to Crouch End Hill. The next time I saw Arthur, when he was back in the world again, I told him we had explored the whole length of the line. He became quite excited.

'Have you now? All of it? It's beautiful, isn't it? Did you see the foxgloves? There must be a mile of foxgloves up there. And the mimosa? You wouldn't suppose mimosa could stand an English winter and I don't know of anywhere else it grows, but it flourishes up there. It's sheltered, you see, sheltered from all the frost and the harsh winds.'

Arthur spoke wistfully as if the frost and harsh winds he referred to were more metaphorical than actual, the coldness of life and fate and time rather than of climate. I didn't argue with him about the mimosa, though I had no doubt at all that he was mistaken. The line up there was exposed, not sheltered, and even if it had been, even if it had been in Cornwall or the warm Scilly Isles, it would still have been too cold for mimosa to survive. Foxgloves were another matter, though I hadn't seen any, only the hogweed with its bracts of dirty white flowers, garlic mustard and marestail, burdock and rosebay, and the pale leathery leaves of the coltsfoot. As the track grew rural again, past Mount View, hawthorn bushes, not mimosa, grew on the embankment slopes.

'It belongs to Haringey Council,' Arthur's voice was always vibrant with expression and now it had become a drawl of scorn and contempt. 'They want to build houses on it. They want to plaster it with a great red sprawl of council houses, a disfiguring red naevus.' Poor Arthur's writing may not have been the effusion of genius he seemed to believe, but he certainly had a gift for the spoken word.

That August his annual novel was due to appear. Liz had been given an advance copy and had duly read it. Very much the same old thing, she said to me: Kallinarth, the hero-king in his realm composed of cloud; Valaquen, the maiden who sleeps, existing only in a dreamlife, until all evil has gone out of the world; Xadatel and Finrael, wizard and warrior, heavenly twins. The title this time was *The Fountains of Zond.*

Arthur came to dinner with us soon after Liz had read it, we had three other guests, and while we were having our coffee and brandy I happened to say that I was sorry not to have any Drambuie as I knew he was particularly fond of it.

Liz said, 'We ought to have Xadatel here, Arthur, to magic you some out of the fountains of Zond.'

It was a harmless, even rather sympathetic, remark. It showed she knew Arthur's work and was conversant with the properties of these miraculous fountains which apparently produced nectar, fabulous elixirs or whatever was desired at a word from the wizard. Arthur, however, flushed and looked deeply offended. And afterwards, in the light of what happened, Liz endlessly reproached herself for what she had said.

'How were you to know?' I asked.

'I should have known. I should have understood how serious and intense he was about his work. The fountains produced – well, holy waters, you see, and I talked about it making Drambuie . . . Oh, I know it's absurd, but he *was* absurd, what he wrote meant everything to him. The same passion and inspiration – and muse, if you like, affected Shakespeare and Arthur Kestrell, it's just the end product that's different.'

Arthur, when she had made that remark, had said very stiffly. 'I'm afraid you're not very sensitive to imaginative literature, Elizabeth,' and he left the party early. Liz and I were both rather cross at the time and Liz said she was sure Tolkien wouldn't have minded if someone had made a gentle joke to him about Frodo.

A week or so after this there was a story in the evening paper to the effect that the Minister for the Environment had finally decided to forbid Haringey's plans for putting council housing on the old railway line. The Parkland Walk, as the newspaper called it. Four and a half miles of a disused branch of the London and North-Eastern Railway, was the way it was described, from Finsbury Park to Highgate and at one time serving Alexandra Palace. It was to remain in perpetuity a walking place. The paper mentioned wild life inhabiting the environs of the line, including foxes. Liz and I said we would go up there one evening in the autumn and see if we could see a fox. We never did go, I had reasons for not going near the place, but when we planned it I didn't know I had things to fear.

This was August, the end of August. The weather, with its English vagaries, had suddenly become very cold, more like November with north winds blowing, but in the last days of the month the warmth and the blue skies came back. We had received a formal thank-you note for that dinner from Arthur, a few chilly lines written for politeness' sake, but since then neither sight nor sound of him.

The Fountains of Zond had been published and, as was always the case with Arthur's, or Blaise Fastnet's, books, had been ignored by the critics. I supposed that one of his depressions would have set in, but nevertheless I thought I should attempt to see him and patch up this breach between us. On 1 September, a Saturday, I set off in the afternoon to walk along the old railway line to his house.

I phoned first, but there was no answer. It was a beautiful afternoon and Arthur might well have been sitting in his garden where he couldn't hear the phone. It was the first time I had ever walked to his house by this route, though it was shorter and more direct than by road, and the first time I had been up on the Parkland Walk on a Saturday. I soon saw what he had meant about the crowds who used it at the weekends. There were teenagers with transistors, giggling schoolgirls, gangs of slouching youths, mobs of children, courting couples, middle-aged picnickers. At Northwood Road boys and girls were leaning against the parapet of the bridge, some with guitars, one with a drum, making enough noise for a hundred.

I remember that as I walked along, unable because of the noise and the press of people to appreciate nature or the view, that I turned my thoughts concentratedly on Arthur Kestrell. And I realized quite suddenly that although I thought of him as a close friend and liked him and enjoyed his company. I had never even tried to enter into his feelings or to understand him. If I had not actually laughed at his books, I had treated them in a light-hearted cavalier way, almost with contempt. I hadn't bothered to read a single one of them, a single page of one of them. And it seemed to me, as I strolled along that grassy path towards the Stanhope Road bridge, that it must be a terrible thing to pour all your life and soul and energy and passion into works that are remaindered in the bookshops, ignored by the critics, dismissed by paperback publishers, and taken off library shelves only by those who are attracted by the jackets and are seeking escape.

I resolved there and then to read every one of Arthur's books that we had. I made a kind of vow to myself to show an interest in them to Arthur, to make him discuss them with me. And so fired was I by this resolve that I determined to start at once, the moment I saw Arthur. I would begin by apologizing for Liz and then I would tell him (without revealing, of course, that I had so far read nothing of his) that I intended to make my way carefully through all his books, treating them as an *oeuvre*, beginning with *Kallinarth, the Cloudling* and progressing through all fifteen or however many it was up to *The Fountains of Zond*. He might treat this with sarcasm, I thought, but he wouldn't keep that up when he saw I was sincere. My enthusiasm might do him positive good, it might help cure those terrible depressions which lately had seemed to come more frequently.

Arthur's house stood on this side, the Highgate side, of Crouch End Hill. You couldn't see it from the line, though you could get on to the line from it. This was because the line had by then entered its valley out of which you had to climb into Crescent Road before the Crouch End Hill bridge. I climbed up and walked back and rang Arthur's bell but got no answer. So I looked up at those Gothic lattices as I had done on the day Liz was with me and though I didn't see Arthur's face this time, I was sure I saw a curtain move. I called up to him, something I had never done before, but I had never felt it mattered before, I had never previously had this sense of urgency and importance in connection with Arthur.

'Let me in, Arthur,' I called to him. 'I want to see you. Don't hide yourself, there's a good chap. This is important.'

There was no sound, no further twitch of curtain. I rang again and banged on the door. The house seemed still and wary, waiting for me to go away.

'All right,' I said through the letterbox. 'Be like that. But I'm coming back. I'll go for a bit of a walk and then I'll come back and I'll expect you to let me in.'

I went back down on the line, meeting the musicians from Northwood bridge who were marching in the Finsbury Park direction, banging their drum and joined now by two West Indian boys with zithers. A child had been stung by a bee that was on one of the buddleias and an alsation and a yellow labrador were fighting under the bridge. I began to walk quickly towards Stanhope Road, deciding to ring Arthur as soon as I got home, to keep on ringing until he answered.

Why was I suddenly so determined to see him, to break in on him, to make him know that I understood? I don't know why and I suppose I never will know, but this was all part of it, having some definite connection, I think, with what happened. It was as if, for those moments, perhaps half an hour all told, I became intertwined with Arthur Kestrel, part of his mind almost or he part of mine. He was briefly and for that one time the most important person in my world.

I never saw him again. I didn't go back. Some few yards before the Stanhope bridge, where the line rose once more above the streets, I felt an impulse to look back and see if from there I could see his garden or even see him in his garden. But the hawthorn, small birches, the endless buddleia grew thick here and higher far than a man's height. I crossed to the right hand, or northern, side and pushed aside with my arms the long purple flowers and rough dark leaves, sending up into the air a cloud of black and orange butterflies.

Instead of the gardens and backs of houses which I expected to see, there·stretched before me, long and straight and raised like a causeway, a green road turning northwards out of the old line. This debouching occurred, in fact, at my feet. Inadvertently, I had parted the bushes at the very point where a secondary branch left the line, the junction now overgrown with weeds and wild shrubs.

I stood staring at it in wonder. How could it be that I had never noticed it before, that Arthur hadn't mentioned it? Then I remembered that the newspaper story had said something about the line 'serving Alexandra Palace'. I had assumed this meant that the line had gone on to Alexandra Palace after Highgate, but perhaps not, definitely not, for here was a branch line, leading northwards, leading straight towards the palace and the park.

I hadn't noticed it, of course, because of the thick barrier of foliage. In winter, when the leaves were gone, it would be apparent for all to see. I decided to walk along it, check that it actually led where I thought it would, and catch a bus from Alexandra Palace home.

The grass underfoot was greener and far less worn than on the main line. This seemed to indicate that fewer people came along here, and I was suddenly aware that I had left the crowds behind. There was no one to be seen, not even in the far distance.

Which was not, in fact, so very far. I was soon wondering how I had got the impression when I first parted those bushes that the branch line was straight and treeless. For tall trees grew on either side of the path, oaks and beeches such as were never seen on the other line, and ahead of me their branches met overhead and their fine frondy twigs interlaced. Around their trunks I at last saw the foxgloves and the tansy Arthur had spoken of, and the further I went the more the air seemed perfumed with the scent of wild flowers.

The green road – I found myself spontaneously and unaccountably calling this branch line the green road – began to take on the aspect of a grove or avenue and to widen. It was growing late in the afternoon and a mist was settling over London as often happens after a warm day in late summer or early autumn. The slate roofs, lying a little beneath me, gleamed dully silver through this sleepy, gold-shot mist. Perhaps, I thought, I should have the good luck to see a fox. But I saw nothing, no living thing, not a soul passed me or overtook me, and when I looked back I could see only the smooth grassy causeway stretching back and back, deserted, still, serene and pastoral, with the mist lying in fine streaks beneath and beside it. No birds sang and no breeze ruffled the feather-light, golden, downy, sweet-scented tufts of the mimosa flowers. For, yes, there was mimosa here. I paused and looked at it and marvelled.

It grew on either side of the path as vigorously and luxuriantly as it grows by the Mediterranean, the gentle swaying wattle. Its perfume filled the air, and the perfume of the humbler foxglove and tansy was lost. Did the oaks shelter it from the worst of the frost? Was there by chance some warm spring that flowed under the earth here, in this part of north London where there are many patches of woodland and many green spaces? I picked a tuft of mimosa to take home to Liz, to prove I'd been here and seen it.

I walked for a very long way, it seemed to me, before I finally came into Alexandra Park. I hardly know this park, and apart from passing its gates by car my only experience of it till than had been a visit some years before to take Liz to an exhibition of paintings in the palace. The point in the grounds to which my green road had brought me was somewhere I had never seen before. Nor had I ever previously been aware of this aspect of Alexandra Palace, under whose walls almost the road led. It was more like Versailles than a Victorian greenhouse (which is how I had always thought of the palace) and in the oblong lakes which flanked the flight of steps before me were playing surely a hundred fountains. I looked up this flight of steps and saw pillars and arches, a soaring elevation of towers. It was to here then, I thought, right up under the very walls, that the trains had come. People had used the line to come here for shows, for exhibitions, for concerts. I stepped off on to the stone stairs, descended a dozen of them to ground level and looked out over the park.

London was invisible, swallowed now by the white mist which lay over it like cirrus. The effect was curious, something I had never seen before while standing on solid ground. It was the view you get from an aircraft when it has passed above the clouds and you look down on to the ruffled tops of them. I began to walk down over wide green lawns. Still there were no people, but I had guessed it likely that they locked the gates on pedestrians after a certain hour.

However, when I reached the foot of the hill the iron gates between their Ionic columns were still open. I came out into a street I had never been in before, in a district I didn't know, and there found a taxi which took me home. On the journey I remember thinking to myself that I would ask Arthur about this curious terminus to the branch line and get him to tell me something of the history of all that grandeur of lawns and pillars and ornamental water.

I was never to have the opportunity of asking him anything. Arthur's cleaner, letting herself into the Gothic house on Monday morning, found him hanging from one of the beams in his writing room. He had been dead, it was thought, since some time on Saturday afternoon. There was a suicide note, written in Arthur's precise hand and in Arthur's wordy, pedantic fastion: 'Bitter disappointment at my continual failure to reach a sensitive audience or to attract understanding of my writing has led me to put an end to my life. There is no one who will suffer undue distress at my death. Existence has become insupportable and I cannot contemplate further sequences of despair.'

Elizabeth told me that in her opinion it was the only review she had ever known him to have which provoked poor Arthur to kill himself. She had found it in the paper herself on that Saturday afternoon while I was out and had read it with a sick feeling of dread for how Arthur would react. The critic, with perhaps nothing else at that moment to get his teeth into, had torn *The Fountains of Zond* apart and spat out the shreds.

He began by admitting he would not normally have wasted his typewriter ribbon (as he put it) on sci-fi fantasy trash, but he felt the time had come to campaign against the flooding of the fiction market with such stuff. Especially was it necessary in a case like this where a flavour of epic grandeur was given to the action, where there was much so-called 'fine writing' and where heroic motives were attributed to stereotyped or vulgar characters, so that innocent or young readers might be misled into believing that this was 'good' or 'valuable' literature. There was a lot more in the same vein. With exquisite cruelty the reviewer had taken character after character and dissected each, holding the exposed parts up to stinging ridicule. If Arthur had read it, and it seemed likely that he had, it was no wonder he had felt he couldn't bear another hour of existence.

All this deflected my thoughts, of course, away from the green road. I had told Liz about it before we heard of Arthur's death and we had intended to go up there together, yet somehow, after that dreadful discovery in the writing room of the Gothic house, we couldn't bring ourselves to walk so close by his garden or to visit those places where he would have loved to take us. I kept wondering if I had really seen that curtain move when I had knocked at his door or if it had only been a flicker of the sunlight. Had he already been dead by then? Or had he perhaps been contemplating what he was about to do? Just as Liz reproached herself for that remark about the fountains, so I reproached myself for walking away, for not hammering on that door, breaking a window, getting in by some means. Yet, as I said to her, how could anyone have known?

In October I did go up on to the old railway line. Someone we knew living in Milton Park wanted to borrow my electric drill, and I walked over there with it, going down from the Stanhope Road bridge on the southern side. Peter offered to drive me back but it was a warm afternoon, the sun on the point of setting, and I had a fancy to look at the branch line once more, I climbed up on to the bridge and turned eastwards.

For the most part the leaves were still on the bushes and trees, though turning red and gold. I calculated pretty well where the turn-off was and pushed my way through the buddleias. Or I thought I had calculated well, but when I stood on the ridge beyond the hedge all I could see were the gardens of Stanhope

Road and Avenue Road. I had come to the wrong place, I thought, it must be further along. But not much further, for very soon what had been a causeway became a valley. My branch line hadn't turned out of that sort of terrian, I hadn't had to climb to reach it.

Had I made a mistake and had it been on the *other* side of the Stanhope Road bridge? I turned back, walking slowly, making sorties through the buddleias to look northwards, but I couldn't anywhere find that turn-off to the branch line. It seemed to me then that, whatever I thought I remembered, I must in fact have climbed up the embankment to reach it and the junction must be far nearer the bridge at Crouch End Hill than I had believed. By then it was getting dark. It was too dark to go back, I should have been able to see nothing.

'We'll find it next week,' I said to Liz.

She gave me a rather strange look. 'I didn't say anything at the time,' she said, 'because we were both so upset over poor Arthur, but I was talking to someone in the Highgate Society and she said there never was a branch line. The line to Alexandra Palace went on beyond Highgate.'

'That's nonsense,' I said. 'I can assure you I walked along it. Don't you remember me telling you at the time?'

'Are you absolutely sure you couldn't have imagined it?'

'*Imagined it?* You know I haven't any imagination.'

Liz laughed. 'You're always saying that but I think you have. You're one of the most imaginative people I ever knew.'

I said impatiently. 'Be that as it may. I walked a good two miles along that line and came out in Alexandra Park, right under the palace, and walked down to Wood Green or Muswell Hill or somewhere and got a cab home. Are you and your Highgate Society friends saying I imagined oak trees and beech trees and mimosa? Look, that'll prove it, I picked a piece of mimosa, I picked it and put it in the pocket of my green jacket.'

'Your green jacket went to the cleaners last month.'

I wasn't prepared to accept that I had imagined or dreamed the green road. But the fact remains that I was never able to find it. Once the leaves were off the trees there was no question of delving about under bushes to hunt for it. The whole northern side of the old railway line lay exposed to the view and the elements and much of its charm was lost. It became what it really was, nothing more or less than a ridge, a long strip of waste ground running across north London, over Northwood Road, over Stanhope Road, under Crouch End Hill, over Vicarage Road, under Crouch Hill, under Mount View, over Mount Pleasant Villas, over Stapleton Hall, under Upper Tollington Park, over Oxford Road, under Stroud Green Road, and so to the station at Finsbury Park. And nowhere along its length, for I explored every inch, was there a branch line running north to Alexandra Palace.

'You imagined it,' said Liz, 'and the shock of Arthur dying like that made you think it was real.'

'But Arthur wasn't dead then,' I said, 'or I didn't know he was.'

My invention, or whatever it was, of the branch line would have remained one of those mysteries which everyone, I suppose, has in his life, though I can't say I have any others in mine, had it not been for a rather curious and unnerving conversation which took place that winter between Liz and our friends from Milton Park. In spite of my resolutions made on that memorable Saturday afternoon, I had never brought myself to read any of Arthur's books. What now would have been the point? He was no longer there for me to talk to about them. And there was another reason. I felt my memory of him might be spoiled if there was truth in what the critic had said and his novels were full of false heroics and sham fine writing. Better feel with whatever poet it was who wrote:

I wept as I remembered how often thou and I

Have tired the sun with talking and sent him down the sky.

Liz, however, had had her interest in *The Chronicles of Kallinarth* revived and had reread every book in the series, passing them on as she finished each to Peter and Jane. That winter afternoon in the living room at Milton Park the three of them were full of it, Kallinarth, cloud country, Valaquen, Xadatel, the lot, and it was they who tired the sun with talking and sent him down the sky. I sat silently, not really listening, not taking part at all, but thinking of Arthur whose house was not far from here and who would have marvelled to hear of this detailed knowledge of his work.

I don't know which word of theirs it was that caught me or what electrifying phrase jolted me out of my reverie so that I leaned forward, intent. Whatever it was, it had sent a little shiver through my body. In that warm room I felt suddenly cold.

'No, it's not in *Kallinarth, the Cloudling*,' Jane was saying. 'It's *The Quest of Kallinarth*. Kallinarth goes out hunting early in the morning and he meets Xadatel and Finrael coming on horseback up the green road to the palace.'

'But's that not the first mention of it. In the first book there's a long description of the avenue where the procession comes up for Kallinarth to be crowned at the fountains of Zond and . . . '

'It's in all the books surely,' interrupted Peter. 'It's his theme, his leitmotiv, the green road with the yellow wattle trees that leads up to the royal palace of Quephanda . . . '

'Are you all right, darling?' Liz said quickly. 'You've gone as white as a ghost.'

'White with boredom,' said Peter. 'It must be terrible for him us talking about this rubbish and he's never even read it.'

'Somehow I feel I know it without reading it,' I managed to say.

They changed the subject. I didn't take much part in that either, I couldn't. I could only think, it's fantastic, it's absurd, I couldn't have got into his mind or he into mine, that couldn't have happened at the point of his death. Yet what else?

And I kept repeating over and over to myself, he reached his audience, he reached his audience at last.

Activities

The Garden of Time

Background notes

J. G. Ballard, born in 1930 in Shanghai, China, of English parents, is one of the foremost writers of Science Fiction and Fantasy in the world. He has published a vast range of stories and novels, a number of which have been filmed. His work is particularly remarkable for its inventiveness and imagination. Much attention has recently been focussed on his work because of the film of his autobiographical novel, *Empire of the Sun* about his childhood in the Second World War.

Pair work

Try to agree on your initial view of the story.
☐ How did the Garden survive for so long?
☐ Can you explain the ending of the story?

Group work

Think about the following questions in relation to the story and discuss them in your group.
☐ Can you suggest where the rabble army come from?
☐ What do we learn about them from the story?
☐ Are they a threat to the couple in the garden or are the couple a threat to them? Prepare notes on your views and report back to the class.

Written assignments

1 Imagine that through some freak of time you wandered into the garden in the story. Using the atmosphere and mood of Ballard's story describe your visit; you might include an encounter with Axel and his wife.
2 The image of the garden is a powerful one in the cultures and religions of many countries and Ballard draws on this tradition here. Using your imagination write your own story or description of a garden; you might use a garden that you have some idea about from a particular source e.g. Eden, the Hanging Gardens of Babylon etc. or you might create somewhere entirely original.

The Fog Horn

Background notes

Ray Bradbury, born in Waukegan, Illinois in 1920, is one of the most accomplished and prolific writers in the genres of Science Fiction, Fantasy and Horror. A number of his stories and novels have been made into television series and films. He has a most inventive and challenging imagination and the special ability to write stories full of adventure and incident that are also intelligent and thought-provoking.

Pair work

1 Try to agree on your initial view of the story.
☐ Who are the two men at the lighthouse?
☐ What do we know of them and their feelings about this experience?
2 Look through the story together carefully and note down details about each character. In particular, why do you think that McDunn remains a keeper after this experience?
3 Imagine that a version of the story somehow reaches the rest of the world. One of you is an investigative journalist who has come to interview McDunn, the other plays McDunn himself. Improvise the interview.

Group work

Think about the following questions that arise from the story and discuss them in your group.
☐ Do any of you believe in the existence of huge, dinosaur-like monsters in our modern world?
☐ Does Loch Ness really have such a monster?
☐ Whether you believe in them or not, what explains humanity's fascination with these lost monsters?
☐ If such a monster were discovered how do you think it would be treated by the media, the military, scientists, etc?

Written assignments

1 Imagine that McDunn and the narrator meet again a few years in the future and they talk about that night; perhaps there have been some developments since then? Write down their conversation as a script, either for a radio or a television play.

2   It is easy to write a horror story about a monster but far more challenging to create a story that evokes our pity and sympathy. Write your own fantasy story involving a 'monster' of some kind; one which will make readers think and feel rather than simply shudder.

3   Most stories that deal with 'monsters' could immediately be placed in the horror genre but this one, even though the monster commits an act of destructive violence, is far from a horror story. Elements of horror stories are used, an atmosphere of suspense and fear for example, but the mood is one of sadness. It is a tribute to Bradbury's skill as a writer that readers are left with a powerful feeling of sympathy towards this lonely creature. Is Bradbury really writing about people rather than dinosaurs? Is he more concerned with the loneliness that we all experience than with a 'monster'? Describe your own reactions to the story.

The Wife's Story

Background notes

Ursula Le Guin is one of the most versatile writers of Science Fiction and Fantasy and she has produced a considerable range of both types of writing. She has managed the difficult feat of making her work appeal both to the young and to older readers. She was born in California in 1929 but her best work has all been produced since the 1960s. Her work has been marked by its innovative nature and by her successful broadening of the subject matter of Fantasy and Science Fiction. She was one of the first female fantasy writers to become famous and to extend the horizons of the genre to include a female perspective.

Pair work

Try to agree on your initial view of the story.
☐   At what point does the reader become aware that we are seeing the events through the eyes of a wolf?
☐   Why does Le Guin include details of the courtship and family life of the wolves? What difference do these make to the overall effect of the story?

Group work

1   The scene in the story where the 'man' is brought down and killed by the wolves just hints at the violence and the gory nature of what

happens. Would it have been a more powerful story if this scene had been described in vivid detail? What is more effective, to leave horror to the imagination or to create a convincing and 'realistic' picture?

2   Imagine that a television company is thinking of a making a series of half-hour films for a new fantasy series. The director cannot decide whether to include this story or not, partly because they are unsure about how much violence to include. What would the group's advice be? Would this story make a good film and how should the final scene be portrayed.

Written assignments

1   It is most unusual to find a story that gives a very well worn subject, the werewolf, such an original and thought-provoking twist. Ursula Le Guin not only manages this but also gives a new depth to a story that is usually full of gory description and nothing more. Choose a familiar creature from the fantasy of horror genres and write your own story changing the typical perspective.

2   Werewolves, vampires, ghosts etc. etc. the list of frightening creatures goes on. Where do they come from? Did they once have some kind of real existence? Are they simply products of the imagination. Why are they so popular in books and films?

Select one mythical creature and trace its history by doing some research about the origins of your chosen creature. Do all the reference books agree about the origins of your chosen creature? Write your own entry for a book on mythical creatures, perhaps you could write with a primary school audience in mind.

Sing a Last Song of Valdese

Background notes

Karl Wagner is an American writer and editor who worked for many years as a psychiatrist. He has published a range of stories and novels and edited the work of other fantasy writers. His works are closely interlinked and the character Kane, featured in *Sing a Last Song of Valdese*, appears throughout them.

Pair work

1   Try to agree on your initial view of the story.
☐   Who is the figure of Kane and is he on the side of evil or good?

☐ How does Korjonos manage to bring all the guilty men together on that night?

☐ How can you explain the effect that Kane had at the end? Korjonos seems to be defeated and somehow Kane aided him: how?

☐ Is justice done at the end of the story?

2 Work together on writing a summary of the story in the form of a legend or song. Include all the main events and characters and make the language you use as true to the story as you can.

Group work

Imagine that you have been asked to work as an advisory group on this story. A movie company are thinking of making a version of the story as a film. They plan to expand the story-line, to include more about all the characters, but still to use the story of Valdese and Korjonos as the central one. They want you to advise them on whether you think this would make a good film for the older teenage market. They would like some suggestions about how they might develop the story-line.

Written assignments

1 Some readers might say that this story was typical of fantasy stories in being full of violence, 'magic' and little else. If you think that this story offers these things and more, write an essay about fantasy stories and why you feel that they are worth reading. Try to explain what they have to offer and use this story and some others you have enjoyed as examples.

2 Kane is obviously travelling in disguise to carry out some dangerous undertaking. Look at the details about him given in the story making notes as you read through. Then combining these with your imagination write the story of Kane's mission.

The Test of the Twins

Background notes

Margaret Weis is from Independence, Missouri, and now lives in Wisconsin. She has worked in publishing, written a great many books, most of them for younger readers, and is now fiction editor for TSR Inc. which publishes many of the most popular fantasy books in America. She has written a number of the stories in the various adventures of Caraman and Raistlin. Will the weaker brother's jealousy ruin his success? Will such opposites as represented in the brothers be able to combine as one force or will they be forever at odds?

Pair work

Try to agree on your initial view of the story.
☐ Each take one of the twins and look through the story for details of them as individuals and as partners.
☐ Each of you should then make a list of their attributes and characteristics and then compare the two lists.
☐ Do the brothers emerge as opposites?

Group work

Think about the following questions that arise from the story and discuss them in your group.
☐ One major theme of this story is the rivalry that can exist between brothers. Do you feel that the relationship of these twins is changed by the test?
☐ Are all brothers and sisters to some extent rivals, do they develop different characteristics or do they influence each other?
☐ Is it an advantage or a disadvantage to be an only child?
Prepare your answers as a report for the class.

Written assignments

1 'There is trouble coming upon us that the world may not survive,' says Par-Salian early in the story. Write a further adventure for the twins once that 'trouble' has begun. Will they be different now that Raistlin has passed the test? How will they cope with the knowledge that they both now have of Raistlin's ambivalence towards his brother?
2 Rivalry between members of the same family or between friends is a familiar and powerful theme in many stories. Write your own story that concentrates on this area of experience.
3 Margaret Weis is a very experience writer of fantasy stories yet she only shows us a glimpse of Raistlin's test – the section where he attacks his brother. What do you think made her leave out most of the test and instead concentrate on the events leading to it and on its last moments? Would you have written the story differently? Try writing a new version of the story in which the test itself is the main event.

Spinning the Green

Background notes

Margaret Elphinstone lives in Scotland where she works on her two chief interests, writing and gardening. She has published stories and poems and has recently completed a novel; she has also co-written a book on gardening, *The Holistic Gardener*. She wrote *Spinning the Green* as a kind of antidote to the numerous traditional fairy tales and legends that exist and which are so frequently read to children.

Pair work

Try to agree on your initial view of the story.
☐ Work through the story together, noting down all the elements it contains that you would both say were from traditional folk and fairy tales.
☐ Can you give reasons why the author has used them in her story?
☐ Tilly's final action is clearly important. What decision does she actually make and how can you explain it?

Group work

The lines that recur in the story:

> 'Who else is there now
> Can spin the green
> To cover the earth anew?'

are very important to understanding the message of the tale. See if you can agree on the nature of that message and, if you can, then consider whether the author is right in putting it forward? Who does she think can now save the earth and why is the idea of 'green' so vital?

Written assignments

1   Many people have argued that the stories we read as children have a deep impact on our minds, so deep that we may not even know that such an influence is there.

A particular concern for many is the way traditional stories represent the roles of men and women; for example the princesses are always beautiful, but have to be rescued by the strong prince before they can marry and live happily ever after.

What are your own views on this topic, do the stories we read as children affect us in this limiting way? Perhaps you might also consider whether future generations will be any different in this respect.

2   Choose a 'traditional' story (or stories) and rewrite it in some way to give it a new and different meaning. You might list stories that you know or look at some children's books and think about the message contained within such stories. Can you keep the basic story but change its message?

The Mist on the Moor

Background notes

Diana L. Paxson lives in Berkeley, California, and has written both fantasy novels and short stories. She has recently completed a trilogy of novels about an imaginary land called Westria. Her short stories have become well known because of her heroine Shanna who appears in this story and is typical of '*Sword and Sorceress*' style heroines who have no truck with female stereotypes.

Pair work

Try to agree on your initial view of the story.
☐   What are the tests that Shanna undergoes and what do they seem designed to prove?
☐   Does Shanna have the qualities of a heroine?
☐   Make notes on Shanna as you look through the story together and examine what we learn about her from the events of the story.
☐   Is she more or less like a heroine after the tests?

Group work

Fantasy stories used to be written mainly by male authors and read by a male readership but now there are significant numbers of female writers and readers. Is Shanna as a female at the centre of the story as an example of this change or does she seem like a typical male hero with a woman's name? Do you think fantasy writing appeals equally to both sexes?

Written assignments

1   Imagine that Shanna carries on with her journey and arrives at a friendly castle where she is well looked after. She is asked by her host

to tell something of her story. Write what she says, either basing it on *The Mist on the Moor* or inventing other adventures that are hinted at in the story.

2   Ama and Yod seem to have a particular role to play in helping people discover things about themselves. Write two conversations between them, one before Shanna arrives and once after she has moved on. Think about their true selves in contrast to the characters that they 'play'.

The Smallest Dragonboy

Background notes

Anne McCaffrey is a particularly well known author of fantasy novels and stories of which she has published a great number over the last twenty years. She is an American but now lives in Ireland. Her work is quite varied and includes Science Fiction, but she is best known for her *Dragon* series. This series contains both novels and short stories and centres on the world described in *The Smallest Dragonboy*: it has been a very popular series, though accused by some critics of being sentimental.

Pair work

Try to agree on your initial view of the story.

☐   How is Keevan's world organized? What do we learn of his training and preparation to be a Dragonrider?

☐   What will his life be like after he has Impressed his dragon?

Group work

Think about the following questions that related to the story and discuss them in your groups.

☐   Does this story take us to a 'typical' fantasy world? What features does the story have that might make it seem typical?

☐   What are the strengths or weaknesses of fantasy? Do fantasy stories help us to escape the real world or to reflect on it through their strangeness?

☐   Do you think that fantasy stories can be considered as serious literature?

Written assignments

1   Retell the story from Beterli's point of view? Look at the story again first to ascertain what we know of his life and character. Does he have any reasons for his bullying attitude towards Keevan?
2   Tell the story of Keevan's first adventure with Hern in the world of Pern.
3   Where are the dragons now? Do they exist only in the imagination or did they once live in the real world? Write a newspaper article about a new discovery concerning dragons, perhaps a group has been found living on a remote island, perhaps a skeleton is found etc. Your report could include interviews with scientists, historians, children etc. – perhaps even a dragon.

Kid Cardula

Pair work

Try to agree on your initial view of the story.
☐ Look through the story and establish how the author gradually informs us of Kid Cardula's real origins.
☐ How does this growing realization add to the humour of the story?
☐ What kind of a character is Manny?
☐ How important is he to our enjoyment of the story?

Group work

1   Think about the following questions that arise from the story and discuss them in your group.
☐ Stories about vampires come from a long oral and literary tradition. In this century such stories have become even more famous through television and film. What do you think is the appeal of these stories?
☐ Why should there have been, for example, so many films made about Count Dracula?
2   If a film company were thinking of making yet another vampire film what would your advice be about what kind of film it should be? How should they treat the subject of vampires and which age audience should they aim for?

Written assignments

1   The author takes a very familiar figure from the horror tradition and uses him to write a clever and amusing story. Try writing a story of

your own that takes a familiar character or situation from the horror genre but which uses a comic style.

2   How is it that we always know more about Kid Cardula than Manny does? He tells the story, he is the narrator, but we understand the Kid, when he does not. Look over the story again at the way the writer has told us what happens through Manny's limited view. Having thought about the way the story it told, continue Manny's tale now that he has another boxing prodigy on his hands.

The Green Road to Quephanda

Background notes

Ruth Rendell is famous throughout the English speaking world for her crime and mystery stories and novels. She published her first novel *From Doon with Death* in 1964 and since then she has published a great range of novels and stories and has won numerous awards. As well as publishing under her own name she has used the pseudonym Barbara Vine.

Pair work

Try to agree on your initial view of the story.

☐ What do we know about Arthur Kestrell? Look through the story together and note down what we learn about him and also your own views on the cause of his death.

☐ Could the narrator have saved Arthur? He describes himself as his friend, yet he never read a single one of his books.

☐ If he had taken more interest would that have helped?

☐ Should he have forced his way in on that Saturday afternoon?

Prepare a short statement for the rest of the class about whether you feel he was to blame in any way for Arthur's death.

Group work

1   Think about the following points that arise from the story and discuss them in your group.

☐ In the review of Arthur Kestrell's book the writer says he wants to 'campaign against the flooding of the fiction market with such stuff'. He goes on to explain his special reason: 'innocent or young readers might be misled into believing that this was *good* or *valuable* literature.' Do you think that there is some truth in what the reviewer is saying, i.e. that fantasy fiction is bad for you! Or would you defend it as generally valuable reading?

2   Prepare a list of pros and cons about the value of fantasy writing.

Written assignments

1   Using a combination of your imagination and the details of the story write a letter in reply to the review of Arthur's book in which you defend both his work and that of other fantasy writers. You might use other writers from this collection as examples in your argument.

2   This story is partly about the ghost of a place. Try writing your own story which involves a special and significant place. Perhaps you might look again first at the careful way in which Ruth Rendell builds up a clear picture of the rest of the area, i.e. the disused railway line and then brings in the supernatural place almost casually. Another striking feature of the story is the narrator's continual emphasis on the fact that he is an unlikely person for such an experience; you might consider using this idea in your own work.

Extended activities

1   Many of the stories in this collection involve violence of one sort or another. Is Fantasy a genre that inevitably covers violent subjects? Consider some of the fantasy stories you have read here and elsewhere; is violence an important part of the writing?

2   Who reads Fantasy and how popular is it? Design a survey to find out who reads Fantasy in your age group and also what other readers think about it. You might contact your local bookshop and library to discover how popular they think Fantasy is and on what basis they stock and display it. You could then uses all this information to write a report about the popularity of Fantasy amongst teenage readers.

3   Many science fiction stories and many horror stories have been turned into films but fantasy films are comparatively rare. Find out from your friends whether they have seen any films that they would classify as Fantasy. What defines a 'fantasy' film? Write an essay about Fantasy films explaining which ones you think are interesting and why.

4   Are fantasy stories simply about action or do they have full and interesting characters? Write about some of the characters who have interested you in these stories.

5   *Kid Cardula* is unusual in making us laugh at what is normally a subject for horror. Try writing your own fantasy story in which you send up the normal style of writing.

Wider reading

This section provides you with some suggestions for further reading and also some ideas for assignments on this reading that you might want to use as a part of your work at school.

Assignments

The following are general suggestions for work.

1 Read the stories or novels of any individual author who has interested you and trace his or her development as a fantasy writer.

2 Select two fantasy novels by different authors that might be compared by theme or subject matter.

3 Pick two or three texts published in the same year. Are they similar because of the time in which they were written?

4 How do male and female Fantasy authors compare? Choose one text from a female and one from a male author and see if you think there are genuine differences in the way they write about men and women.

5 Choose a range of texts and use them to define what good Fantasy writing means to you.

Other books by writers in this anthology

J.G. Ballard

The Voices of Time Everyman 1984 (short stories)
The Drowned World Everyman 1962 (novel)
The Terminal Beach Everyman 1984 (novel)
Vermilion Everyman 1985 (novel)

Ray Bradbury

The Stories of Ray Bradbury Vol 1 and 2 Granada 1983 (short stories)
Fahrenheit 451 Granada 1984 (novel)
The Martian Chronicles Granada 1980 (novel)
Something Wicked This Way Comes Granada 1984 (novel)

Margaret Elphinstone

Spinning the Green comes from a collection called *Despatches from the Frontiers of the Female Mind*, Women's Press, who have also published a number of women writers whose work includes fantasy novels and short stories.

Ursula Le Guin

The Compass Rose Grafton Books (short stories)
Orsinian Tales (short stories)
The Winds Twelve Quarters vol 1 and *vol 2* (short stories)
The Left Hand of Darkness (novel)
City of Illusions (novel)
Threshold (novel)
A Wizard of Earthsea (novel)

Anne McCaffrey The *Dragon* series includes:
Dragonflight, Dragonquest, Whitedragon and also for younger readers:
Dragonsong, Dragonsinger and *Dragonstar*.

Jack Ritchie

Kid Cardula appears in another anthology, *Fantastic Creatures*, edited by Isaac Asimov.

Ruth Rendell

Live Flesh Arrow 1987
A Fatal Inversion (under the name of Barbara Vine) Penguin 1988
Collected Short Stories

Karl Wagner

Night Winds (short stories) Hodder 1979
Darkness Weaves with Many Shades
Death Angel's Shadow
Bloodstone Hodder 1977
Dark Crusade Hodder 1981

Margaret Weis

This story comes from the *Dragonlance* series which at present has three titles, *The Magic of Krynn, Kender Gully Dwarves and Gnomes* and a forthcoming fourth volume. Also of interest are *Dragonlance Chronicles* and *Dragonlance Legends*. These are all published by Penguin.

Fantasy stories by other writers

All titles are novels unless otherwise stated.

Marion Zimmer Bradley

The Shattered Chain Arrow 1978
The Ruins of Isis Arrow 1980

Charlotte Perkins Gilman

Herland The Women's Press 1979

Tanith Lee

Death's Master
Sabella or the Bloodstone
Dreams of Dark and Light: the Great Short Fiction of Tanith Lee (short stories)

Doris Lessing

Canopus in Argos: Archives
The Marriage Between Zones Three, Four and Five
The Sirian Experiments Granada 1982
The Making of the Representative for Planet 8 Granada 1983

Joanna Russ

Picnic on Paradise
The Female Man The Women's Press 1985
The Adventures of Alyx The Women's Press 1985

James Tiptree Jr. (also writes as Alice Sheldon and Racoona Sheldon)

Up the Walls of the World
Brightness Falls From the Air
The Starry Rift Sphere 1988
10,000 Light Years from Home